JACK SHIAN AND THE MAPA MUNDI

JACK SHIAN
AND THE
MAPA MUNDI

Book 2 in
The Shian Quest Trilogy

ANDREW SYMON

BLACK & WHITE PUBLISHING

First published 2014
by Black & White Publishing Ltd
29 Ocean Drive, Edinburgh EH6 6JL

1 3 5 7 9 10 8 6 4 2   14 15 16 17

ISBN   978 1 84502 706 3

Back cover artwork and inside Mapa Mundi illustrations by Rossi Gifford.

A CIP catalogue record for this book is available
from the British Library.

ALBA | CHRUTHACHAIL

Typeset by RefineCatch Limited, Bungay, Suffolk
Printed and bound by Grafica Veneta S. p. A. Italy

To Maggie, again, and to all those who kept
Otherworld storytelling alive over the years.

Acknowledgements

Ian Black, for all his help and encouragement when writing this book, and to all the people who said they couldn't wait for the second book to come out – thank you.

Contents

Shian (pronounced Shee-an [ʃiː + iən]):

n, the otherworld; creatures living in or coming from the otherworld. Also called daemons, fey, gentry, *daoine matha* [*good men*], portunes, etc. (C. 14; origins debated)

www.shianquest.com

1

My Enemy's Enemy

The third echo was . . . silence?

Silence preceded by a hollow emptiness.

Jack had just enough time to be surprised before his eardrums were hammered by a deafening thunderclap. Jumping in alarm, he clasped his hands over his ears.

Screaming, Lizzie tried to do the same – but too late. A trickle of blood emerged from her right ear, and she cooried into her grandfather.

Jack stared in disbelief as the Blue Hag swayed alarmingly on the small hill she had just climbed. Three times he had watched the old woman as she had shuffled up an incline to perform the ancient Shian ritual for clearing the snows at winter's end. Three times on reaching the top she had drawn her long staff upright and thudded it into the ground. Reverberations in the surrounding hills had melted the snow for fifty yards around her. Or at least they had done so twice. But the third time – nothing.

The staff had hit the ground, just like before. But this time, there was no sound – until the thunderclap. The Blue Hag steadied herself and peered round, perplexed. Her gaze passed over Jack, Lizzie and their grandfather, and came to rest on a much higher hill to Jack's left. He followed her eyes. There, standing at the very summit some two hundred yards away, he could just make out three figures. One of them waved something – a sceptre perhaps? – above his head; and then came the sound of distant cheering. The sky above the figures darkened, there was a crack of thunder, and a single lightning strike scorched a solitary tree on the hillside. Howling curses in their direction, the Blue Hag retreated quickly down the hillside.

"Who in Tua's name are they?" exclaimed Jack. The taste of treachery fouled his throat, like the time he'd realised Rowan had sold out the Congress four months earlier.

Grandpa Sandy had withdrawn his own sceptre from his cloak. Fingering it agitatedly, his stern look was fixed upon the distant figures. Jack saw him clench his jaw.

Lizzie rubbed her right ear and squeaked in alarm as she saw the blood. Cowering behind her grandfather's cloak, she peered fearfully at the distant figures as one of them rose from the ground and did a graceful pirouette in the air. The manoeuvre had lasted fully ten seconds. Grandpa's face relaxed and he lowered his sceptre.

"Kildashie," he said simply, emphasising the second syllable. "I'd almost forgotten what they were like."

Jack looked again at the distant figures, but could make

little out. Then he saw the one with the sceptre wave it in an arc above his head. There was another loud peal of thunder, and it began to rain. Not just ordinary raindrops: huge smudges of water that drenched within seconds.

"Why'd he do that?" complained Lizzie, trying to pull her coat over her head. "I'm all wet. And my ear hurts."

As more thunderclaps resounded around the hills, Grandpa Sandy waved at the figures, beckoning them over. After a short consultation, they began to glide from their hilltop, their cloaks flapping in the wind.

"Are they flying?" asked Jack. They reminded him of the two hags who had flown at the back of the Brashats at Dunvik.

"No, they can't fly." Grandpa kept his sceptre in his hand. "They live on islands far out into the ocean. They use their cloaks to glide."

The three men landed and made their way with effortless haste up towards them. Jack could see that they were all tall, with long, straggly hair that swept about their faces. The one bearing the sceptre was in front, taking huge strides. Within seconds they had reached Jack and the others.

"Shian of Kildashie," said Grandpa Sandy slowly and evenly, "I have not seen you for many years. What brings you so far from your islands?"

Their leader stood, his long sceptre planted firmly on the ground. He gazed long and hard at Grandpa Sandy before replying.

"I am Tig, from Hilta. These are Boreus and Donar. We have come to renew old acquaintances, now the Brashat are vanquished."

"I well remember your dealings with the Brashat." Grandpa

Sandy paused, considering how best to phrase things. "But you should know better than to interrupt the Blue Hag. She will be hard to placate now, and that will prolong our winter."

"What is that to us?" sneered Boreus. "Your sheltered winters are like spring."

Jack squinted up at the rain-sodden sky. Dark clouds swept across the heavens, and the wind howled around them.

"But these are not your islands." Grandpa Sandy pressed his point home. "Here we mark the new spring with this custom. You have disturbed the rhythm of the snow's end."

Boreus growled under his breath and aimed his sceptre at a tree a little way down the slope. There was a flash, and the tree burst into flames. He moved forward menacingly, but was instantly halted by Tig's raised right forearm. Tig turned and muttered to his colleague, who retreated, scowling.

"I apologise if we have over-stepped the bounds of hospitality," said Tig, with an ingratiating smile. "We hope to be able to join you in the celebration of your spring." He looked up at the sky, his brow furrowed briefly, then he waved his sceptre expansively over his head. The skies lightened appreciably. The rain dwindled to little more than a drizzle, and the wind dropped.

Lizzie, impressed, stepped out confidently from behind her grandfather. The ringing in her ears had stopped.

"How did you stop the echo?"

Tig looked sternly at her, and she quickly averted her gaze.

"My granddaughter is eager to learn," said Grandpa Sandy, putting his arm protectively around Lizzie's shoulder.

"There are times for lessons, and times to watch in wonder," said Tig evenly. "We will leave you now. But there is much we need to discuss with your Congress. Tell Atholmor that we wish to see him soon."

Without further word, the three Kildashie turned and strode off. Jack had remained silent since their arrival. As the Kildashie reached the edge of the wood he turned to his grandfather.

"Grandpa, I don't trust them. Stopping the Blue Hag's *infama*, isn't it?"

"*Infama*? You mean against nature?" asked Lizzie.

"You may be right, Jack," said Grandpa. "They're wild, I'll grant you that."

"I got the same feeling as I got with Konan last year." Jack thought back to his first encounter with Konan the Brashat in Edinburgh's High Street in Edinburgh, and their subsequent clash at Dunvik just before the battle.

"They *are* rather uncivilised," his grandfather conceded. "I'd heard rumours that they'd destroyed a lot of trees on their islands; and they don't seem to mind being out in the winter weather, like we do."

"Then they could attack us in the wintertime, when we're all sheltering."

"Well, that's possible; but I think we can manage them. There's only a handful of them. They're also sworn enemies of the Brashat, so you've something in common there."

"Our enemy's enemy?" asked Lizzie.

"How come you've never mentioned them before?" demanded Jack. "And where are these islands?"

"Let's find the Blue Hag first, shall we?" said his grandfather. "We should see if we can't get her on the hills again."

"She went down that way," said Lizzie. "D'you think she'll come back?"

Grandpa led the two youngsters down the hill, but away from the woods into which the Kildashie had vanished. A few minutes later they came upon the Blue Hag. Wrapped in her cloak, she was huddled down, muttering to herself, and fingering a small wooden wheel. Grandpa held up his hand to stop Jack and Lizzie. Slowly he edged forward.

"*Cailleach*," he began, at which she raised her head. "We have seen your power in putting the snows of winter to flight. The Kildashie lack the understanding of your ways, but they have left. Will you continue now?"

The old woman looked at Grandpa Sandy for a moment, then snorted derisively and turned her face away. Grandpa Sandy returned to Jack and Lizzie, and ushered them quickly away.

"We can stay in the bothy tonight. By tomorrow she may have forgotten the Kildashie."

He led the youngsters along the edge of the trees to a small wooden hut.

"Grandpa, d'you really trust the Kildashie?" asked Jack as Grandpa kindled a fire. "I got a bad feeling about them."

"I want to know how they stopped the echo," said Lizzie.

"It must be to do with the wind," said Grandpa. "They live with it."

"I got a funny feeling, like I was empty inside."

"It made my ear bleed," moaned Lizzie.

"The Kildashie *are* strange; their islands are far out into the western ocean. Living in such a bleak place has made them . . . shall we say uncivilised? By reputation, all they fear is another Norse invasion."

"You mean like at Dunvik last year?"

"That's right, Lizzie. And you saw how fierce those warriors could be. But they only came because of the Chalice."

"Do the Kildashie mix with the humans, Grandpa?" queried Jack.

"The humans left the islands many years ago. The living got too tough for them – or maybe the Kildashie did. The Kildashie were forced onto the islands by the Brashat. There's no love lost between them."

Jack thought that he ought to feel more kindly towards the Kildashie, but he didn't.

"There's something about them I don't trust. Controlling sound could be dangerous. And interrupting the Blue Hag, that's wrong, isn't it?"

"What they did was quite impressive. But you're right: breaking the spring rite was *infama*. They should have had more respect."

Jack scowled. The way Boreus had moved towards him had definitely been threatening. Grandpa, however, would hear no more about it, and instead turned to the stories about the Blue Hag.

"Tell us how she becomes young again," pressed Lizzie.

Grandpa smiled at her. "When the last of the snows have gone, the Blue Hag raises her staff aloft and sings out a long note that carries from one hill to the next. When the sound dies away, she is transformed and walks off the hill a beautiful young woman. Then spring has returned. It's the turning of the year – the season wheel has moved on." He paused. "We'll catch up with her tomorrow."

★

The next morning was dismal and damp, which set the pattern for the day. The Blue Hag showed no sign of coming out, and reluctantly Grandpa suggested that they would be as well to return to Edinburgh. Packing their things, they headed back for the low road.

2
Fenrig's Return

Edinburgh Castle lay under a thin blanket of snow.

Life in the Shian square was too quiet. Many inhabitants were away, ushering in the new season with family and friends elsewhere. Jack, after an hour of idly kicking stones, put on his coat and went for a walk along the castle ramparts. Trebling up to human size as he passed through the square's side gate, he emerged next to St Margaret's Chapel. From there he walked around to the ramparts. Few human visitors disturbed the peace of the castle at this time of year; Edinburgh is not at its best in late February.

Jack's frustration at the slow end to winter grew. With Petros and Rana away in Rangie with their parents, it was just Lizzie, Grandpa and himself in the house. Little had happened since the great Hallows' Day battle at Dunvik nearly four months earlier.

Great battle, thought Jack. It had certainly become much

grander in the telling and retelling since. The snows had arrived not long after, and most Shian, according to custom, had retreated indoors for the winter.

Jack liked the firelight parties, the songs and the stories, but he had longed too to get out into the open. When his grandfather had suggested the youngsters accompany him to see the Blue Hag's great spring rite, he had jumped at the chance. Rana had pestered her parents to take them to Rangie for a few days, and Petros had been obliged to go too, for, as Uncle Doonya had put it, there was no way he was being left on his own in the house.

While Petros had decided that Rangie was less likely to be snow-covered than the hills north of Keldy ("a totally uncivilised place," he had said), Lizzie had consented to go with Jack. So it was that their grandfather had taken them north to watch the great spring ritual.

A snowball hit Jack on the side of the face. He spun round angrily, only to find Petros and Rana standing ten yards away, laughing heartily.

"The look on your face!" exclaimed Rana gleefully.

The snow dripped down the inside of Jack's collar. Swiftly, he stooped down and scooped up a handful of snow. Within seconds, the air was thick with snowballs and shouts, and before long all three were both thoroughly warm and covered in melting snow. Flushed with the exertion, Rana called a halt.

"I thought the Blue Hag was going to make the snow disappear," said Petros.

Jack brought them up to date with the story of the Kildashie, and how the Blue Hag was sulking.

"So we didn't miss much," stated Rana.

"Seeing the Kildashie gliding was cool. But they're Unseelie. And they've got some kind of control over sound. I wouldn't trust them; Grandpa says they used to fight against the Brashat."

"Unseelie fighting each other doesn't bother me. In fact, any enemy of the Brashat is probably all right," pointed out Petros. "We're well rid of them."

"Not all of them," whispered Rana, pointing to the side wall of the chapel, where Fenrig stood scowling, his sister Morrigan by his side. Jack, Petros and Rana got to their feet, and for a few moments there was a silent stand-off. Finally, Morrigan spoke.

"C'mon, bro. We'll leave these peasants alone." Quickly she and Fenrig passed through the gate to the square below.

"What're they doing here?" demanded Jack. He'd thought Fenrig and his sister were being kept out of the way while their father, Briannan, was suspended.

"Mum told me," said Rana. "They're going to stay under the castle. Their dad's . . . well, you know. And they haven't got a mother. All the rest of their family got suspended, so there was no one to look after them."

"Fenrig hasn't *got* a mother?" said Jack. "I just thought she was somewhere else."

"Huh, boys," snorted Rana. "You wouldn't take the trouble to find out."

"Grandpa said she wasn't around, but I thought that just meant . . ." Jack's voice tailed off. He realised he knew very little about Fenrig. They had started their apprenticeship together the previous summer, but Fenrig had made it clear from the outset that he wanted nothing to do with the other apprentices.

Jack could see that Petros was unsettled by Morrigan's appearance. Quite apart from her deliberate insult, the knowledge that she could transform into a crow (and that, in this guise, she had nearly eaten him when he had used the beetler disguise at Dunvik) gave Petros the shivers.

"You mean they're going to be under the castle with us?" he groaned. "I knew it was too good to last."

"How come you know about it?" Jack accosted Rana.

"Well, Mum said something about them being orphans and having nowhere to stay."

"So who's been looking after them since Dunvik?" challenged Jack.

"Some of the Elle-folk took them, up to Iceland, I think. But they can't stay there forever. I can't see them fitting in."

"It's not like they fit in here either," pointed out Petros.

"There you are." Their grandfather's voice carried out to them from along the castle ramparts. "I see you've been enjoying what's left of the snow."

"Grandpa, why are Fenrig and his sister here?" asked Jack. "That's asking for trouble."

Grandpa Sandy stopped. He looked down at the three youngsters thoughtfully.

"Petros," he said after a few moments, "your mother would like you and Rana to go and unpack your bags. Would you go and help, please?"

Petros threw Jack a quizzical look, but decided against arguing.

"I need to get out of these wet clothes anyway. Come on, Rana."

"Jack, we can have a little chat, just ourselves. I'll get you dried when we get to the Stone Room."

Jack's eyes opened wide. He had only twice seen the Stone: just after he had arrived under the castle, and once after the fight at Dunvik. The long winter shutdown had meant further visits had been out of the question.

Wordlessly, Grandpa Sandy led Jack to the castle's War Memorial entrance, from where they could see the stairs leading to the Stone Room.

"We'll just wait here a minute," whispered Grandpa, pulling Jack into the darkened doorway. "They'll be finished soon."

Jack's damp clothes clung uncomfortably to his skin. He shivered.

A short while later, a man emerged from the doorway. He turned the key with a flourish, walked smartly across the small square and disappeared into the castle's Great Hall.

"We can go now." Leading Jack by the hand, Grandpa walked up to the locked door. Placing his left hand against it, he whispered, "*Perlignum!*"

Jack felt a sudden lurch as he was pulled forward. Gasping slightly, he saw that he and his grandfather were at the foot of some stairs. They began to climb and soon reached the Stone Room's large security door.

"This one is alarmed," whispered Grandpa. "Stand back a minute."

Grandpa Sandy took out his sceptre and aimed it at the solid steel door. The sceptre's ruby glowed, and Jack was aware of a soft shimmering sound, like far-off thunder. He stared in astonishment as the door melted in front of his eyes. Once they were through, the door reappeared. Jack found that his clothes, suddenly, were dry and warm.

"You haven't come in that way before, have you?" asked Grandpa.

"No. You've only ever brought me up from the square. How d'you make the door disappear?"

"Oh, ways and means. You'll learn them as you get older. I'd better deal with the cameras."

Grandpa Sandy held up his sceptre to the vaulted ceiling, putting the cameras on hold. Then he clicked his fingers, and two chairs appeared by the glass cabinet. Jack had seen the King's Chalice in the cabinet once before, but the sight of it made him catch his breath.

"It does look good in there, doesn't it?" said Grandpa. "The humans are delighted, even if they only get it for half the year."

They settled down into the chairs, and Grandpa began.

"I'm sure you're surprised to see Fenrig. Quite a lot changed at Dunvik: although the Brashat got suspended, there was an agreement that all Shian should have access to the Chalice and the Stone."

"I still don't see why we have to share them with the Brashat," snorted Jack. "They wouldn't share them if they'd won."

"The power of Gosol, Jack, remember. It's about the *goodness* of the creator force. We must do the right thing and for the right reason. Sharing the treasures was part of the agreement; even the Brashat, when the time comes, will be allowed access."

"They were let off lightly. Three years suspended for all they did? They should never be allowed out."

"The Chalice belongs to everyone, Jack. Fair shares. And part of the deal is to take care of Fenrig and his sister. Their whole family is suspended, so they've no one."

"Rana said their mother's dead. Is that right?"

"She died when Fenrig was very young. Like you, he grew up without a mother."

"He still had his father!" Jack shouted.

"I'm sorry: I didn't put that very well. I just meant he's had to cope with loss, like you. I grant you he's charmless, but sometimes there are reasons for these things."

Jack said nothing.

"Anyway, the Congress has decided that we should keep an eye on Fenrig and Morrigan. They wintered with the Elle-folk, but they don't really belong there, so they'll stay in the square. Mawkit's left, but Olbeg and his wife are moving into that house; they'll look after them. Morrigan will work with Gregora the baker, so she'll be with Purdy. Fenrig will continue at Gilmore's."

Jack stared at the contents of the cabinet. He didn't like what he was hearing, and sought some comfort from the Stone and the Chalice.

"Are you getting the Stone's buzz?" asked Grandpa softly.

Jack *was* feeling it: he couldn't deny that the Stone made him feel warm. It was even stronger than when he'd first seen the Stone the previous summer. The Chalice being there seemed to double the effect.

"It's a nice fuzzy feeling. But there's still something missing. What are we going to do about the Sphere?"

"Well, now that winter's coming to an end, we can start again. We couldn't do much once the snows came. The manuscripts Fenrig stole – well, evidently his father took them. We should have established where they were before suspending him."

"And what about my father?" Jack's voice dropped low as he spoke.

"We keep looking. Never give up hope, Jack."

"Can't we go and interrogate Konan?" Jack's mind flitted to the Brashat warrior, now merged with a large oak tree near the cave at Dunvik.

"I don't think that will produce much, unless you can find a way of unlocking the charm that put him there. But you never know." Grandpa Sandy stood up now. "We have the Oestre festival soon. We'll go back to Rangie for that. And we could always consult Tamlina."

Realising that his grandfather wanted to leave, Jack asked, "Can't we stay a bit longer? We've only just got here."

"Another time," replied his grandfather. "We should get back; it'll be supper time. Aren't you hungry?"

Jack *was* hungry, but the prospect of Aunt Katie's cooking was no match for time with the Stone. However, Jack could see that his grandfather was preparing to leave and, reluctantly, he stood up. With a click of his fingers, Grandpa Sandy made the chairs vanish. Holding his sceptre up to the vaulted ceiling, he switched the surveillance cameras on again.

Grandpa then wrapped his cloak around Jack, clutched his sceptre firmly and struck the floor. A red glow was followed by a rushing sense, and Jack found himself next to his grandfather back in the Shian square.

3

Oestre

Within two days the snow was disappearing, leaving behind damp streets and gardens that squelched deliciously: the Blue Hag had resumed her annual ritual. While Lizzie complained that they hadn't got to see the *cailleach* transform, Jack consoled himself that the festival in Rangie was only three days away.

Midsummer was the highpoint of their year for most Shian, but for Jack it was Oestre. Seeing the world come to life again after the winter brought him hope; and this year, it was the hope that he would find his father. The warming air and the lengthening days gave Jack a sense of optimism. Fenrig being back was a drag, but for now he was determined to relish the prospect of the festival at Rangie.

When Jack heard that the Kildashie would be present, he was in two minds. He knew that many different groups had been invited along in recognition of the return of the King's Chalice. The McCools from the west of Ireland had arrived, and the Inari, who had brought rare foods from Japan. But Unseelie? Did the Congress know what it was doing?

Grandpa wouldn't be easily fooled, only . . .

Something gnawed away at Jack's insides, something nameless and troubling.

"How was work today?" asked Aunt Katie brightly as Jack slouched back from his day at Gilmore's.

"Not bad." Jack reached for the jug of tayberry juice.

"Come on, there must be more to it than that," pressed his aunt.

"Fenrig started back. He doesn't look like he wants to be here at all."

"Did you speak to him?" asked Aunt Katie anxiously.

"Not much. He doesn't bother answering."

"Did he tell you about Iceland, then? What were the Elle-folk like?"

Aunt Katie's persistence irritated Jack.

"I don't know," he snapped. "I told you, Fenrig doesn't say much. I don't know why the Congress said he could come back here."

"That's a bit harsh, Jack. You know he has no family left, not since his father was . . . put away."

"His father got off lightly. Three years, it's a joke."

"Jack, I just meant . . ."

But Aunt Katie's words were left to trail in the air, as Jack picked up his satchel and stormed out. He had just determined to go out to the High Street when he saw Petros and his sisters on the other side of the square.

"Hiya Jack," called Rana. "We're just going to get some things for the festival. Want to come?"

Grateful that he had received his apprentice's allowance the day before, Jack joined his cousins as they went to the shop at the top of the square. With the Chalice attracting even more Shian to Edinburgh, the shop had expanded hugely. Jack reached up and grabbed a firework wheel.

"We'll spin it down the hill after the Blue Hag's started spring – to mark the turning of the year."

Petros smiled broadly as he pocketed some forget-me-aye powder.

"It's brilliant," he explained. "It works on Shian *and* humans: you just put some in their drink and they forget who they are. Boyce told me about it."

"That's dangerous," pouted Lizzie. "People do silly things if they don't know who they are. 'Specially humans. Grandpa said you must only pick someone who really deserves it."

"I'll find someone," smirked Petros. "I can't wait for the festival."

"You've only just come back from Rangie," pointed out Jack.

"Yes, and they're really pulling out all the stops for this one," said Rana. "You won't believe how much it's changed. It's been charmed so it looks a lot bigger; they're expecting hundreds."

The youngsters' expectation and excitement carried them through the necessary chores of the next three days. When the time came to leave Edinburgh, they all met up in the front room with Aunt Katie and Grandpa Sandy.

"Have you got everything you need?"

Aunt Katie, as ever, flustered around. Petros smiled back as Jack rolled his eyes.

"Come along, you lot." Grandpa Sandy took control. "All ready? Right, off to the low road. Uncle Doonya's gone ahead with the Congress."

As he led them down towards the low road mound, Jack asked, "Grandpa, how come we can use the low road? I thought we had to walk, like we always do."

"More low roads are opening up. The Chalice and the Stone are having some effect, I can tell you."

When they reached the house down by the foot of the square, Jack saw to his surprise that it was no longer gloomy. Freshly painted and with clean curtains in the windows, it bore little resemblance to the ramshackle house it had been a few months earlier.

Linking arms on the mound, the six huddled in close.

"Wind-flock Rangie!" whispered Grandpa Sandy, and they all began the familiar spinning that announced their entrance onto the low road.

Within two or three minutes they found themselves by the hawthorn tree on the edge of Rangie wood. The air felt sweeter to Jack, and the well-known sounds of the woods were reassuring. But there was more: the hubbub of hundreds of people, music, laughter, chatter, all coming from just down the glen.

Grandpa Sandy led the way, striding purposefully towards the small field that lay between two hills. Naturally sheltered, local farmers favoured it as good pastureland. But Jack could see no trace of sheep or cattle today, and the field itself seemed much larger. Catching his eye, his grandfather said, "Looks different, doesn't it? Well, that's a special Oestre for you. The Congress has made a few adjustments, to make room for all the extra guests."

Though not as many as had been at the previous midsummer's festival at Falabray, the extra guests, as Grandpa called them, were numerous.

"Are we going to slow down time again tonight?" asked Jack breathlessly.

"There's no need. Rangie is so sheltered there's little chance of humans turning up. Just to make sure, we've got charms to keep them away. In fact, we move in the other direction tonight: we'll use Fugitemp."

"'Fugitemp'?"

"Time speeder, Jack. Our time will go quickly: it makes things even better for us. For the humans it will pass as usual."

Grandpa moved off to talk to Atholmor. Next to them Jack saw Uncle Doonya in conversation with Armina the enchantress. Approaching them, Aunt Katie called out, "There you are. We'll let the kids off to see what's going on. How are you, Armina?"

As she and Armina engaged in conversation, Uncle Doonya turned to the youngsters.

"Here's some spending money. Try and make it last longer than an hour, Rana. We've got ages yet."

"Come on, I've heard there's Phooka here," said Petros. "Let's see who can find them first."

"Just a minute," said Jack. "I'll just give your mum my firework wheel to look after."

Rana and Lizzie ran off excitedly into the crowd, while Petros steered Jack towards one of the many food stalls.

"Aren't we going to find the Phooka?"

"Time for that later. Let's get some heather wine first."

Jack looked round cautiously, wondering if his aunt or uncle could see them.

"Don't worry about Mum and Dad. They'll never see us in this crowd."

"Maybe later. I don't feel like any now."

"Suit yourself," sniffed Petros. "I'll catch up with you at the Phooka stall, yeah?"

Mumbling assent, Jack set off to investigate what the festival had to offer.

Rana came running up.

"There's Flame spirits!" she announced breathlessly. "Come on! Lizzie's keeping a space for you. She asked a Kildashie to do a sound trick, but he just walked away."

The sky had already darkened, and the Flame spirits glimmered in the evening gloom. As the night darkened, they performed a series of tricks: floating, transforming into hares or rabbits, exploding into showers of light. Jack sat entranced as they performed one trick after another. After the disappointment of the Falabray festival, it was good to see what they could do.

Petros appeared after a while and tried to get Jack to come and see a Ghillie-Doo fire carnival, but Jack shrugged him away. Petros retreated sulkily, and later Jack saw him sitting alone with a goblet of what he suspected was heather wine.

Jack wandered among the different Shian. Almost everyone had been invited: there were korrigans and Phooka, pisgies and Elle-folk. And the Kildashie: about thirty of them, tall and wild-looking, a little apart from the main throng, but not excluded. Jack wasn't surprised that Lizzie's request had been rebuffed. They were making their own entertainment round a huge fire – *They must've cut down at least three trees to make that!* – wild dances, and songs that were both soothing and frightening. They used whistles and drums, and the polished horn of what must have been an enormous ram. Jack decided to steer clear of them.

They were creating quite a mess too. Jack heard Tig shouting at Boreus for throwing his rubbish into the stream. The word 'poison' – or was it 'pollution'? – drifted over. Boreus was angry, but seemed reluctant to challenge his leader.

Unseelie, thought Jack. They don't like humans; they don't even like each other; and they certainly don't respect this place.

The entertainment continued, though. The Inari, from Japan, played screeching, jangly music that made Jack's spine tingle; the pisgies flew in formation, re-enacting battle scenes; and the McCools sang mournful songs of loss and parting.

"Their songs *are* beautiful," said Grandpa, moving beside Jack. "They sailed here, you know. They conjure boats when they need them, and they sailed right round Scotland to get here. Look, one of them gave me a charm stone for calling the boats."

He showed Jack a small emerald with a tiny flaw in it. Held up to the firelight, the flaw looked like a minute ship. Grandpa slipped the gemstone into his pouch.

The night passed quickly. Grandpa had been right: the fun *was* concentrated, but disappointingly it seemed no time at all before the first glimmers of daylight brightened the eastern horizon.

"Olwen's coming," whispered Aunt Katie to Jack as he sat watching the eastern sky.

Jack knew the story, but had never been present when the Blue Hag, in her new spring form, had arrived.

I didn't get to see her transform, but this is the next best thing. Olwen at the Oestre festival means spring is finally here.

It was going to be a good year; Jack just knew that. He got his firework wheel ready.

As the sun crept above the skyline of the hill, the Blue Hag came into view, holding aloft her staff. Despite the sun being at her back, her face shone: Jack had never thought a face could change so much. And she began to sing: clear notes, a slow ascending scale that drifted over. The hairs on Jack's neck stood on end, and as the scale ended and a peaceful stillness settled over the crowd, a glow enveloped the old woman. Jack's whole scalp tingled as the transformation hit him: Olwen. He had never seen such a beautiful young woman before.

Without warning, there was an angry cry from behind him, and Jack saw Olwen point her staff directly towards him. Shian turned to look at him . . . no, not him, behind him. Jack turned round and saw the Kildashie group, all gathered together. They were standing, poised. Jack saw Boreus with his sceptre drawn, directing it up towards Olwen.

"No, Boreus!" commanded Tig.

But it was too late: a bolt flew up towards the woman on the hill. With a loud *crack!* the bolt hit her staff, and it exploded.

The next few minutes were pandemonium.

4

Fallout

With a screech, Olwen flew down to the field, her staff smouldering. Tig ordered two Kildashie to disarm Boreus, and he was quickly held, but this wasn't enough. An angry crowd gathered around the Kildashie, brandishing their sceptres. Hexes started to fly, and two Kildashie fell, screaming in pain. Atholmor's pleas for restraint fell on deaf ears as hexes and bolts were fired and returned.

Olwen tried to barge her way through to where Tig was attempting to keep order, but Donar had cast a protective charm around him. People were shouting, there were screams of pain as hexes found their mark, and a deafening peal of thunder echoed around the hills.

And suddenly, silence.

Jack felt icy cold. Out of the corner of his eye, he had seen his grandfather wave his sceptre in an arc above his head. It was as if he had thrown a cover over an unruly caged bird;

from a squawking, arguing chaos, out of the blue there was calm. It was freezing, but it *was* calm. Jack could see, he could hear, but he couldn't move a muscle.

Grandpa Sandy lowered his sceptre slowly, making sure that his encasing hex was holding. He stepped forward and touched Olwen on the arm. She came to life, and with horror Jack watched her age in front of him. Her face began to wrinkle, her skin sagged and her lustrous brown hair showed flecks of grey. Alarmed, Grandpa Sandy removed his hand from her arm. Her ageing stopped abruptly, and she became immobile once more.

Grandpa Sandy pondered this for a few moments, then reached into his jacket pocket and withdrew a small stone. Placing this first in Olwen's right hand, he touched her arm again; once more she came to life, and the ageing Jack had witnessed slowly reversed itself. Within a minute she had returned to her youthful state, but she was docile, and Jack saw his grandfather lead her away from the crowd. When they were about twenty yards away, Grandpa Sandy waved his arm over Olwen's head and she simply disappeared.

Walking through the motionless crowd, Grandpa Sandy trailed his sceptre on the ground, creating a thin line of fire. Then, retreating and facing the whole crowd, he directed his sceptre in the air, firing a single bolt. The crowd parted: the Kildashie to one side of the line and everyone else to the other side. The separation complete, the sceptre was raised again. Jack watched his grandfather wave his arm expansively over his head and dissolve the encasing hex.

The arguments began afresh as the crowd found it could move and speak again, but without the violence that had gone before.

"There will be no hexing at this festival!" roared Atholmor, holding up his hand for silence. "You were invited to demonstrate that Seelie and Unseelie can live in peace! Men of Kildashie, you are summoned to appear before the Congress to answer for your actions."

Tig approached the invisible wall.

"We *do* come in peace. But Boreus thought he was being attacked. The Blue Hag was going to fire at him."

"You fool!" cried Atholmor. "She is no longer the Blue Hag — she is Olwen; her staff has no hex power. The snows have gone, and the *cailleach*'s powers of force with them."

"Then Boreus will atone for what he has done." Turning round to Boreus, Tig ordered, "You will stay in the house of Atholmor as his bonded servant for seven years!"

Boreus started to protest, but was silenced instantly by a blow to his temple from Donar.

"And what use is an unconscious servant to me?" enquired Atholmor sarcastically. "The Kildashie council will attend the Congress this evening at Cos-Howe. Now go, and prepare your defence well."

Tig nodded. He gave orders to Donar, and the two of them ushered the Kildashie away. They turned and left the field silently, carrying the motionless figure of Boreus. As the group reached the edge of the woods at the foot of the glen, they melted into the trees.

Jack felt a wave of nausea sweep over him, a delayed reaction to the skirmish.

What is it about the great festivals? First midsummer, now this. The Unseelie can't ever be trusted!

The sick feeling gave way to anger, and Jack turned on his grandfather.

"I told you there was something wrong with them! They've ruined everything!" he shouted. "I didn't even get to use my firework wheel!"

"That's enough!" Aunt Katie barked. "We'll just go home. Pierre, you come along with your father in a while. I'll take the young ones."

Pierre: Uncle Doonya's real name. When used in front of the children, it always meant things were serious. As indeed they were. Jack, half shocked at his outburst, felt salty tears well up as Aunt Katie led him and the others down to the low road entrance. Lizzie looked nervously at him, unsure of what to say, but Rana had no such qualms.

"Well, that didn't help," she spat. "We could've stayed and got breakfast from the korrigans."

"Come on now." Armina strode up behind them. "Back home. This is not the time or the place."

Jack found himself trotting beside Armina as she strode down towards the hawthorn tree. Rana and Petros followed on, with Lizzie urging her mother to join them. Wiping her eyes, Aunt Katie followed, and within a minute they were on the mound of earth that marked the low road. Armina stretched her long arms around them all and whispered, "Wind-flock castle!"

Jack woke at midday. Like the others, he had gone to bed when they'd got home. Now he was hungry, but wasn't sure if it was safe to go downstairs. Uncle Doonya had returned home a few minutes after Jack and the others, loudly making known his displeasure at that morning's events. Jack knew he shouldn't have shouted at his grandfather, especially in front of so many people.

But I was right about the Kildashie. They're dangerous; everyone can see that now.

There was no sound from Rana and Lizzie's bedroom next door. Jack looked across to where Petros lay, snoring gently. He had gone to sleep complaining of a headache, but not before he'd threatened Rana with dire consequences if she "explained" matters to their parents.

He's not waking for a while, but I'm hungry now.

Jack listened as hard as he could, but could make out no sounds from below. He crept downstairs and pushed open the kitchen door. It squeaked horribly, and Jack's heart leapt as he saw his aunt and uncle sitting at the table.

"It's all right, Jack; come in."

Unconvinced by his uncle's calm tone, Jack advanced cautiously into the kitchen, leaving the door open behind him.

"Sit down, Jack dear. I'll get you some lunch," said Aunt Katie kindly.

"I was just going," said Uncle Doonya, rising to his feet. "I'll see you all later. There are things we need to clear up with Grandpa."

As Jack ate his lunch, he watched his aunt. She had the haunted look he'd seen in her eyes the previous autumn, just before they'd all gone up to Dunvik.

The quiet was broken by Rana and Lizzie, who came in from the square.

"Guess what we heard!" shouted Lizzie, her face flushed with excitement.

"I'm telling; it was me who found out," pouted Rana. "Freya told me her dad said that some of the Congress want the Kildashie to be suspended."

Jack smiled at the thought. "Serves them right. They can rot there forever."

Rana, however, had different ideas.

"They're wild, but not evil. The Brashat got suspended for stealing the King's Chalice, and for trying to kill us. A fight over Olwen trying to hex one of them isn't the same."

"There's something very dangerous about stopping the Blue Hag's echo," said Aunt Katie. "They destroyed an awful lot of trees in Rangie, and there's even rumours about them controlling the weather. Now come along, out of the house, you lot. And quietly: Petros is sleeping."

Exchanging knowing looks, Rana and Lizzie made their way out to the square. Jack followed them, at a bit of a loose end without Petros.

"Come on up to the High Street," said Rana, dragging him over to the Shian gate. "We've something to show you."

A chilly wind hit them as they emerged onto the castle esplanade above. For a moment Jack wondered about going back for a thicker coat, but Rana pressed him to continue.

"Bet you've never been to the End of the World, have you?" she asked teasingly.

Mystified, Jack looked at her. They'd gone past St Giles' Cathedral, and were almost at the corner where the road to the right led to Falabray.

"Purdy's friends with one of the Cos-Howe boys," said Lizzie, "and he's playing in the match against Claville. It's in

Edinburgh this year. If we play our cards right, we might be able to see the match."

"Where do they play?" asked Jack.

"Near Cos-Howe usually, but this year it's the High Street. The castle's one goal, and Holyrood Palace gate is the other. And if we go over there," Rana pointed across to the Finisterre café-bar, "we should be able to see the match."

"Grandpa showed me that place once, but how d'you see the match? At least in Claville we were up high. Even on the top of that building you can't see more than a tiny bit of the High Street."

"They've got some special screens inside. It's like the humans with their cameras: different ones for different parts of the High Street."

"How come you know all this?" asked Jack, vexed that his younger cousins knew more than he did.

"Purdy told Freya, and she told us."

"And can they really get us in OK? It's a human pub too, isn't it? They don't allow you in unless you're eighteen."

"It's not just a human pub, silly," pointed out Rana. "It's part Shian. We haven't found out how to get in yet, but we're working on it. It'll be nice to see the French players again."

Jack recalled how Rana and Lizzie had been captivated by one of the Claville players after the match the previous summer.

"Bit old for you, wasn't he?" he asked mischievously.

Rana's punch to his arm was swift and painful. Jumping back to avoid further attack, Jack bumped into his grandfather.

"There you are."

Jack started. Had he been there all the time, listening to their conversation?

"I'm glad I caught up with you. Something quite remarkable has happened. Don't worry, Jack," he added, seeing the dismay on his grandson's face. "This morning's spat is forgotten. The Kildashie have presented us with a problem, but the Congress will handle that. Something else has happened, to do with the Stone, and that's got some Congress members in a tangle."

"Petros isn't feeling well," announced Rana. "D'you want to know why?"

"I don't want to hear sneaky tales, if that's what you mean. Now, let's get back home; we've things to discuss." He turned back up towards the castle.

Lizzie looked across at Jack, mouthing, 'What's up?'

Jack shrugged. If it was the Kildashie, it wasn't going to be good news, he was sure of that.

5

Lessons with Finbogie

Within a few minutes the whole family were gathered together. Uncle Doonya looked pensive, but Jack couldn't decide what he was thinking. Petros appeared looking dishevelled and complaining of a dry throat.

"What I'm telling you now must not be repeated to anyone, do you understand?" Grandpa looked round the room. "Last night, while we were at the festival, Daid went up to the Stone Room. At midnight he felt a change in the air; the glass cabinet glowed and then disappeared for a minute. He was able to reach forward and touch the Stone."

There was a moment of silence while the enormity of this sank in.

"Are you sure it's not just one of Daid's stories, Grandpa?" asked Petros. "You know how he ... well, you know, he sometimes overdoes things."

A giggle escaped Lizzie's lips.

"But the special glass they use in the cabinet: you said Shian couldn't break that," pointed out Jack.

"That's just it: he didn't break it. And I wouldn't be telling you if I hadn't checked. At times today the glass is permeable. I myself have been up to the Stone Room and touched the Stone."

"What about all the humans? Aren't they going in and out as well?" queried Lizzie.

"The stairs leading to the Stone Room have been damaged," said Grandpa mischievously. "Visitors won't be allowed up while they're deemed unsafe."

"Can we all go up and see it, then?" asked Jack, his excitement rising.

"That's where we meet our first problem," said Grandpa pensively. "The Congress – some of them anyway – are terrified that the Stone will be taken if word gets around. That's why you're not to breathe a word of this to anybody."

"You'd better tell them about Daid," said Uncle Doonya.

"Ah yes. In his excitement, Daid was a little unguarded and came back to the square shouting about what had happened. Luckily, hardly anyone was around, but the secret may already be out."

"Where's Daid now?" asked Rana.

"I'm afraid that for his own safety, Murkle has had to take Daid in. It's vital that we don't allow this to become common knowledge until we check what it all means."

"So he's been locked up, has he?" asked Jack. "Like a prisoner?"

"Because of what happened this morning, we must be careful. Tig has taken control of his more impetuous colleague, but you were right to distrust the Kildashie – they are Unseelie, after all. Daid might not be safe from them."

"Why are you telling us, then, if it's such a big secret?" asked Petros gruffly.

"Others may have overheard Daid last night, and they may tell you. But now you know to keep it quiet. This is dangerous."

"What's the Congress doing about the Stone?" asked Jack urgently.

"The Congress doesn't want everyone traipsing in to the Stone, if that's what you mean. The Darrig and his friends are standing guard; nobody will get past them."

"I'm sure it'll all settle down soon." Aunt Katie's voice had more hope than belief.

"So what're we supposed to do then?" asked Petros grumpily.

"Stay on your guard. Tell us if you hear anything unusual." Grandpa Sandy looked sternly at all the youngsters in turn. "And we can do a little searching ourselves. We could see what Tamlina makes of all this. She was helpful last year. That's where you youngsters come in. She seemed to take to you."

"She hexed me, Grandpa," pointed out Petros. "Bloody sore it was, too."

"But she asked your forgiveness as well. And she knows Jack and the girls. We'll decide after the Congress meets tonight."

Jack saw his aunt wipe a tear away as she turned and silently left the room.

"With Murkle looking after Daid, you may just have to continue with your apprenticeships in the afternoon," said Uncle Doonya. "But don't forget to keep your eyes and ears open. And for goodness' sake, don't mention any of this to Fenrig or his sister."

"I know they don't like us much," said Rana, "but they might at least have come along to the festival."

"Olbeg thought it best to keep them away, since the Kildashie were going. It's just as well they weren't there when the hexes started flying," answered Grandpa. "The Brashat and Kildashie are sworn enemies."

Jack's antipathy towards Fenrig was not lessened by this knowledge.

I don't trust the Kildashie, but a well-aimed hex at Fenrig wouldn't be that bad.

Jack waited impatiently for news from the Congress. His grandfather and uncle had gone off before suppertime, but even by the time the youngsters were sent to bed, they'd heard nothing. Petros, having regained his usual good humour, speculated on the reasons for the lack of news.

"Country boys, those Kildashie; the Congress should send them back to whatever windswept rocks they come from."

"But if it's so obvious, why's the Congress taking so long?"

Jack didn't sleep well, and the next morning his head felt muggy. Petros, however, was bright and optimistic as they headed down for breakfast.

"The Congress will have sent them packing. D'you fancy coming up to the High Street after lessons?"

Helping himself to some toast, Jack shrugged.

"Did your dad come back last night, then?"

As he spoke the front door opened, and they heard Uncle Doonya and Grandpa Sandy. Aunt Katie, who had been distractedly wiping some dishes, dropped a saucer, uttering a squeak of alarm.

"It's all right." Grandpa's voice was tired, but he looked relaxed. "We've had a very long time of it, and there's lots to tell you. But you youngsters need to get going to your work. Gilmore and Cormac will be wondering where you are if you don't get a move on."

"But Grandpa," protested Jack, "you've got to tell us what happened."

"There's not enough time now. But one thing you do need to know: Finbogie has been asked to teach self-defence to all of the apprentices. He'll start this afternoon with the youngest ones. Jack, go to his house after lunch. Daid's still ... indisposed."

"But Finbogie hates apprentices. He wanted us all put away last year," pointed out Petros.

"All the same, he knows about protecting himself. And he's been asked to teach all of you."

"Are the Kildashie making trouble, then?" asked Jack quietly. "We wouldn't need self-defence classes if there was no threat."

"Like Grandpa said, we can discuss things this evening. Now, off to your work."

As Jack and Petros left, they heard Rana and Lizzie coming downstairs.

"Save yourselves the bother," he said flatly, indicating the kitchen door. "Right now we don't need to know."

It would do no good, he knew. Telling Rana and Lizzie not to do something guaranteed that they would do it.

Gilmore was irritated that morning. Jack knew it wasn't

just his poor stitching or Fenrig's non-appearance. Everyone in the square seemed tense, as if something bad was about to happen. Freya and Doxer could throw no light on things. For Freya this was unexpected, but she clearly had no more information about the Stone or the Kildashie.

After lunch, Jack set off for Finbogie's house. Boyce glowered as he approached. Jack saw Diana, Purdy and Suque whispering to one another, while Lee-Brog and Séan played with some cards.

"Can't we go in?" asked Jack, breaking the silence.

"I'm keeping as far away from him as I can," snarled Boyce. "He hexed me and my sister for no reason at all last year. He's just a bad-tempered old . . ." His voice broke off as he became aware of a figure standing behind him.

"Bad-tempered old what?" asked Finbogie evenly.

Boyce didn't reply. He blushed and stared at the ground.

"In you come, the lot of you." Finbogie's voice brooked no disobedience. His face, scarred from ear to mouth, had a disconcertingly lop-sided look.

Dutifully, the seven youngsters filed into his house and made their way to his spacious front room. None, however, dared to sit down. Finbogie followed them in and took his place in a large armchair that sat by the fireside. A portrait of an elderly man scowled down at the room.

"You are here," stated Finbogie flatly, "because the Congress wishes to preserve your lives. We are currently obliged to entertain certain people – Unseelie people – who do not share our way of doing things and who may well be dangerous. For this reason you all need to learn how to defend yourselves."

He looked around the room. The seven apprentices

remained standing, awkwardly. None dared to look straight at him.

"Some of you may have noticed my slight facial disfigurement . . ."

Jack coughed, suppressing a laugh. *Like you could miss it!*

"Which only goes to show – life can be dangerous. But there should be more of you." Finbogie's tone was calm, but carried no hint of warmth whatsoever. "Where are the others?"

"Fenrig's not here," stated Jack. "Sometimes he doesn't turn up."

"Ah yes, the Brashat boy. I'll deal with him. But there's one more."

The apprentices looked at each other, but nobody seemed to have a response. Eventually Purdy spoke.

"Kaol's not here either. I don't know where she is."

"Hmmph. Well then, to start you off, you will all copy out the fifty most common defence hexes. In your best handwriting. You can share these three books. There's paper and pencils over there."

Finbogie indicated a wooden box on a polished table by the window and casually dropped three books on the floor.

Clutching a piece of paper and a pencil, and not daring to lean on Finbogie's immaculate table, Jack squatted down and opened one of the books on the floor. *Morven's Book of Defence*, said the cover. Jack looked up the chapter on hexes and began to copy out from the book. Lee-Brog and Séan joined him.

What's the point of this? After ten minutes of scratching a pencil across the thin paper, Jack was seething. *Practical lessons are what we need.*

Muttering curses under his breath, he looked up and saw that Lee-Brog and Séan were thinking the same.

If Finbogie was aware of the apprentices' thoughts, he was not bothered by them. He sat and watched as the youngsters completed their task over the next forty minutes, but made no comment until he was satisfied that they had all finished.

"Right," he said coldly. "You are to take your papers and learn the first twenty-five by next week. After that you'll learn the rest. I've got to get all of you lot prepared as soon as possible. Don't disappoint me. Now, out with you. I've work to do."

He ushered the apprentices out. Stiff from kneeling for so long on a hard, cold floor, Jack was glad to get out and stretch his legs. Predictably, the apprentices' moans had started.

"That was torture . . ."

"Never again . . ."

"Being attacked's got to be better than that . . ."

Despite their common experience, Jack didn't feel like sharing with the others just now.

I need some air. I'll see what's doing down the High Street.

He walked over to the far side of the Shian square, and placed his left hand on the rock wall.

Effatha! The gate sprang open, and Jack swelled to human size as he stepped smartly onto Edinburgh Castle's esplanade.

6

Challenging the Congress

Jack fumed as he walked down the High Street.

Any more lessons like that and someone's going to die.

Pausing to peer into one of the High Street tourist shops, he became aware of someone standing just behind him. His mind flashed back to the previous summer: Konan the Brashat had accosted him right here. Suddenly panicked, he spun round, only to find his cousin Ossian there.

"You gave me a fright," spluttered Jack. "I didn't know you were coming down today. Didn't you use the low road?"

"Dad wanted to try the humans' bus. It's really slow."

"I've been on a human bus," said Jack. "Petros took me once, around the city. It stops at all the important buildings and stuff."

"This one stopped a lot, but no' at important buildin's."

Jack's thoughts turned to his Aunt Dorcas's superior cooking. "Did your mum bring any baking?"

"Sure. She's over there." Ossian indicated over the road. "We saw you lookin' into the shop. It's noisy, eh?"

"And cold," said Jack, shivering. "Brrr! It was warm a few minutes ago. Have you brought the cold weather with you?"

Jack looked across the street to where Uncle Hart and Aunt Dorcas were standing talking. *Someone's with them*, he thought. The cold feeling turned icy as he recognised Boreus.

"What's he doing here?" gasped Jack. "He's a Kildashie. He tried to hex the Blue Hag at the Oestre festival."

"Did he?" Ossian didn't sound too impressed.

"And they stopped her when she was getting rid of the snow. That's messing with nature," urged Jack. "It's dangerous."

Ossian paused. "Dad knows some Kildashie. They don't often leave their islands, but he knows a couple of them, from way back."

Uncle Hart waved across to the two boys. Boreus looked up too, and, seeing Jack, he muttered something and strode off down a side street. Was it Jack's imagination? Had it suddenly got warmer?

Uncle Hart and Aunt Dorcas crossed over the road.

"It's good to see you, Jack. We've come by bus today. Takes a long time." Uncle Hart looked pleased with himself.

"Jack says the Kildashie stopped the Oestre festival," stated Ossian.

"They did," insisted Jack. "And they stopped the sound when the Blue Hag was clearing the snows."

"Did they now?" mused Uncle Hart. "I'll need to discuss that with your grandfather. Shall we go up to the castle?"

Now practised in using the gate on the esplanade, Jack

corralled the three visitors, and soon they were in the Shian square.

"There's Rana and Lizzie," said Ossian, running over to his two younger cousins. Aunt Dorcas and Uncle Hart followed on, still marvelling at the changes in the Shian square since their last visit.

"It's so much busier," Aunt Dorcas kept saying.

Alerted by the sound of Ossian's bellowing hello as he reached Rana and Lizzie, Aunt Katie appeared, and ushered them all in. Aunt Dorcas had recounted for the third time how long the bus had spent queuing in traffic as it made its way into Edinburgh.

"You should just use the low road," said Jack. "It only takes a few minutes."

"I think we'll be going back that way, right enough," conceded Uncle Hart. "I thought it would be an experience, that's all. Now, what's this I hear about the Kildashie? I was just talking to one of them up in the High Street."

"It was Boreus," stated Jack. "When he saw me he took off."

"He's not scared of you," snorted Petros.

"I didn't say he was, just that he left when he saw me. And it got a lot colder when he was there."

"What happened at the Congress last night, then, Dad?" asked Rana. "We waited up for ages."

"Here comes Grandpa now. He'll tell you."

"Last night we discussed the Kildashie's behaviour." Grandpa Sandy spoke gravely. "As you know, they've a careless attitude to their surroundings: they take more than they need from the woods and they create a lot of mess. The attack on

Olwen was the worst they've been. Several members of the Congress were all for banishing, or even suspending, them."

"I know what they did was wrong, Grandpa," pointed out Rana, ignoring her mother's warning look. "But they're not as bad as the Brashat, are they?"

"As it happens, Atholmor agrees with you," replied Grandpa Sandy. "He's calmed down after yesterday morning, and he had a long discussion with Tig. The upshot is that the Kildashie are to stay out of the city for now, along the coast. They have also offered to join forces with us against the Brashat when they are released."

There was a moment's silence.

"But that's crazy," spluttered Jack. "Boreus attacked Olwen. They nearly took us back to winter."

"And Armina said they cut down loads of trees at the Oestre festival," piped up Lizzie. "I know there's loads, but they didn't even use most of what they cut."

"Jack," said Grandpa softly, "some of the Congress just can't face any more fighting, not after the trouble we had last year. For what it's worth, I believe that's foolish; the Kildashie are obviously just as capable as the Brashat of causing trouble."

"And they've got some control over sound," added Lizzie. "That thunderclap made my ear bleed."

"There've been stories about strange silences in town recently," chipped in Aunt Katie. "And it's certainly been chilly. But I'm sure it'll all sort itself out."

She's not even fooling herself, thought Jack.

"We can't go against the Congress," stated Uncle Doonya firmly. "If they've decided that the Kildashie are safe, then we have to accept that."

Grandpa Sandy gave Uncle Doonya an odd look that Jack couldn't decipher.

"Nevertheless," continued Grandpa, "we should be cautious. I propose that Jack and the girls come with me to Keldy. We can leave tomorrow evening. I'm sorry not to be a better host, but this is important."

"I'll come with you," replied Ossian. "The city's no' my thing. No' enough space."

As they filed through to the kitchen for supper, Jack saw Grandpa tug at Uncle Doonya's sleeve, holding him back for a few moments. When they both appeared a few moments later, Uncle Doonya looked angry.

The next day dragged by. Jack's poor tailoring caused Gilmore to stamp his feet in frustration. Freya kept shooting Jack quizzical looks, trying to identify what was wrong. The only one who seemed to be enjoying things was Fenrig. He sneered as Jack dropped pieces of cloth and laughed openly as he fumbled his stitching. Doxer, as ever, was impassive.

At lunchtime, a sniggering Fenrig made his usual quick exit. As Doxer sat and silently ate his sandwiches, Freya tried to get Jack to talk about what was wrong, but Jack just shook his head.

"Can't say. Everyone's just upset because of the Kildashie."

Freya's eyebrow arched. "You're planning something, aren't you? If you won't tell me, I bet Rana and Lizzie will. They're bound to know."

Jack was glad when finishing time came. Without pausing to speak to Freya, he ran out of the workshop.

Rana and Lizzie were sitting outside the house, with a small overnight bag between them.

"Mum's been crying again," stated Lizzie flatly. "She doesn't want us to go. She hasn't said so, but I can tell."

"She'll be all right," said Rana, now evidently used to the idea of leaving Edinburgh for a while. "But why are we going to see Tamlina?"

"Because if there's problems with the Kildashie, she'll know about it," said Ossian.

"She may know what happens in Keldy, but the Kildashie are not from there. Why would she know about them?" queried Rana.

"Because they passed through Keldy to get here," explained Ossian. "Anyway, are you all ready to go?"

"We're just waiting for Grandpa. He said he'd be along soon." Rana poured herself a cup of juice.

"I can take you on ahead," said Ossian impatiently.

"The last time you took us on ahead we ended up in France," stated Jack.

"You enjoyed it, didn't you?" smiled Ossian.

"Yeah, but we got into trouble. Let's just wait for Grandpa."

Their grandfather, however, was some time in coming. "Too many things to do," he'd said when he arrived. Following brief goodbyes, they all set off for the low road. As they climbed up onto the small mound and joined hands, Jack saw Fenrig appear as if out of nowhere. He hadn't time to say anything to his grandfather before they were all enveloped in his large cloak and his grandfather had chanted, "Wind-flock Keldy."

Jack was used to the sensation now, having travelled this way many times. The spinning, the drone that rose to a whine and the keening sound. But this time it was different: the moaning and wailing were much louder. Jack thought back to the times when there'd been a funeral in Rangie. As the corpse was carried along, most of the village would line the road, offering sympathetic cries to the bereaved family. On every other low road trip, Jack had been briefly reminded of this, but now he was hit by a torrent of despair. The air felt colder too, and the low road seemed darker.

What's going on?

After several minutes, the spinning and the droning slowed down, and they all came to rest. Jack looked around. Lizzie's mouth and eyes were still clamped tightly shut. Ossian had already started to walk along the track to his house, but Grandpa remained on the small mound that marked the low road entrance.

"You felt it too, Jack?"

If Jack didn't know better, he would have said his grandfather was worried.

"It didn't feel right," said Jack. "The wailing was louder, and it was colder."

"I know. Let's get up to the house; we can warm up there."

The track was wet, and they were muddy by the time they reached the house.

"We'll need an early night," stated Grandpa as he stood by the fire Ossian had kindled. "So, after supper, it's up to bed. Ossian, can you send a grig and find out if Tamlina's nearby? Wherever she is, we'll have to find her."

"Sure," said Ossian. "Have you got somethin' to pay her?"

Grandpa silently handed over a small silver coin, eyeing Ossian carefully as he did so. Then he retrieved a series of small packages from within his cloak. "Now then, Katie's prepared a snack for our supper."

Jack rolled his eyes.

7

Malevola

The night had been stormy. Twice Jack was woken by the sound of thunder, and when morning finally came he awoke to the sound of rain hammering on the windowpanes. Jack stole quietly downstairs, but he wasn't the first up. Ossian and Grandpa sat in the kitchen, conversing in a low tone. Grandpa gestured for Jack to sit down.

"We're just running over our plans. Have some breakfast, and we'll fill you in."

Jack reached over and helped himself to some bread and heather honey.

"The grig came back early this morning, but she was in a bad state," stated Grandpa, getting up and pacing the room. "The wood creatures are anxious. It's spring, but last night's was a winter storm. The grig could hardly speak, but at least she knows where Tamlina will be today."

"Are the seasons getting mixed up, Grandpa?" asked Jack.

"The Kildashie nearly stopped spring from coming, didn't they?"

"Impossible to say." Grandpa sat down again. "These things happen, from time to time."

"But I've never known it here before," said Ossian solemnly.

Jack had never seen Ossian look less than confident before. Now he sounded . . . *anxious*.

"We've used this grig loads o' times. It's no' like her to get scared."

"Who's scared?" asked Rana, as she and Lizzie entered.

"Never mind," said Grandpa brusquely. "We need to get going. We've got quite a walk to find Tamlina."

"What are we going to ask her, anyway?" queried Lizzie.

"About the Kildashie. And she may tell us more about the Sphere."

"And my father," stated Jack. "I want to know if she's heard more about him."

Ten minutes later found them all leaving the house. The rain was little more than drizzle now, but a windy, dreary kind of drizzle that gets into your bones.

Following the grig's directions, Ossian headed for the clearing where Tamlina would be gathering spring roots. But whereas the previous summer's walk had been a pleasant stroll in the woods, this was a longer, colder journey. Jack started to recognise certain landmarks.

"I remember that tree," he announced. "It's funny, like an old man stooping."

Grandpa Sandy halted and held up his hand. A high wailing sound was just audible. He looked quizzically at Ossian.

"It's the Banshee," said Ossian slowly. His face had gone pale.

Grandpa instinctively pulled Rana and Lizzie closer to him.

"Where is she? Can you tell?"

Jack had been surprised at breakfast to see that Ossian looked concerned; now his cousin was frightened, he was sure of it.

"Who's the Banshee?" Lizzie asked. "What's it mean?"

"It means death is near," said his grandfather carefully. "Stick close together, all of you." He withdrew his sceptre from his cloak and fingered it nervously. "Come on, we must find Tamlina. If she's in trouble, we'll have to help her."

Jack glanced nervously around. All the normal sounds of the wood had disappeared: no small creatures scurrying through the dead leaves, no birds overhead. He gulped: it didn't go down easily, and he had to swallow hard.

They had moved forward a hundred yards when they heard the first *crack!*

"Get behind me, quick," ordered Grandpa, as he hurried for the nearest tree. He crouched down, with the four youngsters copying him.

"It came from over there." Ossian indicated ahead. A series of loud cracks followed. Rana and Lizzie looked nervously at each other, then at their grandfather.

"It's near the clearing, isn't it?" said Grandpa, holding his sceptre out in front of him. "Stay right behind me. I don't want any of you getting hurt."

The sound of cracks grew louder, and there was a sudden shout of pain.

"That's Tamlina, I'm sure o' it!" shouted Ossian. Disregarding his grandfather's cautious approach, he charged forward.

"Come on, Grandpa." Jack gripped his grandfather's cloak and urged him on.

The five ran forward. The cracks had continued, but they were slower now.

And suddenly they saw her: Tamlina, lying in a pool of blood. Propped up against a withered oak tree, she still held her sceptre up. But standing over her was a tall dark-haired woman in a flowing black cloak, cackling evilly. Next to the woman were two creatures: an emaciated old man with a long cap, which he was dipping into the blood; and a tiny demon, like the ones Jack had witnessed at Dunvik. Tamlina's sceptre crackled feebly, but her power was gone. The tall woman stooped down and removed the ring from Tamlina's finger.

"Tamlina!" shouted Ossian. He darted forward and was met full on by the victorious enchantress. A bolt shot from her sceptre and hit Ossian square in the chest. He fell backwards, without a sound.

"No!" Grandpa Sandy fired a hex at the enchantress, but it was like a fly bouncing off a windowpane. She seemed indestructible.

"You dare to fire at me?" she growled, her voice both terrible and exciting. She brandished her own sceptre and fired a swift volley of hexes at Grandpa Sandy.

It was an uneven contest. The hexes flew in too fast for him to respond. The first one hit him on the left shoulder. He spun round, a look of surprise on his face, and his sceptre flew out of his hand. The second (or was it the third?) glanced off his back, and another caught his leg as he fell.

Jack's eyes flashed. In a second he had darted down and scooped up his grandfather's sceptre. Crouching low, he aimed it up at the tall woman.

"*Gosol!*"

A bolt shot from the sceptre, crackling as it flew. A look of amazement spread over the face of the tall enchantress. Jack kept the sceptre steady, although his arms ached; it was as if the bolts weighed a ton. Finally, with a loud *crack!* the woman disappeared. The tiny demon vanished too, but the thin old man was left. He sank to his knees, his hands outstretched as if pleading for mercy. Jack got uncertainly to his feet. The bolts had stopped flying, but it still took all his strength to hold the sceptre.

Shivering, Jack advanced on the old man, who cowered as he approached. Then Jack made his mistake. He glanced round to see if Rana and Lizzie were all right, and in that instant the old man took his bloodstained cap and hurled it at the girls. With a shriek, he vanished.

His screech was echoed by a loud scream from Lizzie as the gory cap narrowly missed her face. Spinning round, Jack could see that the old man had now disappeared, but was uncertain of where he might be hiding. He crouched low, until the sound of his grandfather moaning came to him. Satisfying himself that the creatures were indeed gone, he ran over to where Grandpa Sandy lay. Rana knelt down too and stroked her grandfather's arm anxiously.

"What do we do?" she asked plaintively.

Looking round, Jack saw Tamlina slumped by the oak tree. He ran over to her.

"Tamlina! Can you help Grandpa?"

A thin smile spread across Tamlina's face. Her lips moved, but for a moment there was no sound. Then a hoarse whisper emerged.

"Give him these. On his forehead." Clearly in pain, she indicated a small pouch beside her. Jack looked quickly inside and found three small pebbles. Extracting them, he ran back and carefully placed them on his grandfather's brow.

Lizzie and Rana watched apprehensively. With relief, they saw Grandpa Sandy's eyes open. He blinked, turned to face Jack and mumbled inaudibly. Then, taking the stones from his brow, he levered himself painfully into a sitting position. His left shoulder was steaming gently, and his right leg gave off a bitter burning smell.

"Where's Ossian?" His voice was cracked.

Ossian had not moved since being hit. Sprawling on the ground, his neck was twisted. Grandpa dragged himself over to where Ossian lay. Then, looking over to where Tamlina sat propped against the oak, he called over, "Can you help?"

The thin smile reappeared on Tamlina's face. With exquisite pain, she beckoned Jack over. As he neared, he saw that the pool of blood around Tamlina had grown.

"Will you be all right?" His voice was quiet, uncertain.

Tamlina reached out and took his hand.

"Yer cousin was only bolted," she whispered. "He'll live."

Grandpa Sandy had dragged himself painstakingly over to where Tamlina lay.

"What can we do to help you?" he asked anxiously.

Tamlina shook her head sadly. With a painful gesture she indicated the sticky pool around her.

"The blood is dark; I will die. She took my Raglan."

The Raglan again? She spoke of it last year too! But what does it mean?

Lizzie began to sob, and Rana instinctively put her arm around her distraught sister.

Coming to, Ossian rubbed his chest where the bolt had struck. Wincing, he first knelt, then stood slowly up. Lurching over to the others, he looked down at Tamlina's pale face.

"Who was that?" he demanded. "The other enchantress, who is she?"

"Malevola," croaked Tamlina. "She's Unseelie – from Tula – the north island. She heard o' my Raglan, then o' yer Chalice; now she wants the Sphere." Her voice was almost inaudible.

"What *is* your Raglan?" cried Jack.

"Gosol . . ." Tamlina's voice gave out.

"Raglan is to do with Gosol?" Jack's voice was almost a shout.

"Tamlina, it is urgent." Grandpa Sandy's voice broke through. "The Sphere – where is it? Can you tell us?"

Tamlina's eyes were closing. With an effort, she fought to keep them open.

"Seek ye the cave o' the saint. The giant's bridge . . . when columns awake . . ." She got no further. Her head slumped forward.

"What cave? What bridge?" Jack's voice was plaintive, but it was lost almost immediately in the sound of a loud wail echoing through the trees.

"Jack." His grandfather's voice was little more than a croak. "She's gone. She's at peace now."

Lizzie's sobs grew in intensity, merging with the wail that came from the trees around them.

"Well, we can't leave her here for the crows," said Ossian.

Now almost recovered from the bolt that had laid him out, Ossian began to clear a space between the trees. Jack joined in, brushing away the leaves and the deadwood that littered the ground. Within a few minutes they had cleared a big enough space for Tamlina's body.

"You'll have to lift her over." Grandpa indicated that he could not use his sceptre to raise Tamlina's body from where it remained, slumped against the tree.

Jack looked at Ossian.

"I'll tak' her shoulders." Ossian stooped down and reached his arms through Tamlina's.

Jack tried not to look as a dark stain spread over Ossian's shirt. He shuffled over and gripped Tamlina's legs. Awkwardly, the boys dragged the body over to the clearing they had created. Grandpa beckoned them away.

"You've done well. I'm sorry I couldn't help."

"Won't your sceptre work?" Rana's voice was worried.

"For some things only." Still gasping in pain, Grandpa grasped his sceptre and levelled it at Tamlina's inert body.

"May she rest at peace." His voice was uneven.

Jack looked and saw his grandfather sag to the left. With an effort, Grandpa Sandy steadied himself.

"*Pulviscin!*"

From his sceptre emerged a dim orange beam, which encased Tamlina's body, making it glow. Gradually, it began to smoulder, then became a flame. The body and the clothes burned, but the surrounding ground was untouched by the fire. Within a minute or two there was only a small pile of ash.

The wailing sound stopped.

The sudden stillness unnerved Jack. He looked around nervously, unsure of what to expect.

"It's not safe here," stated Grandpa. "Wherever Malevola went, she may decide to come back." He forced himself onto his feet and began to limp painfully back the way they had come, indicating to the others to follow. Then, stopping, he turned around to Jack and put his hand on the youngster's shoulder.

"Once again, Jack, I have to thank you. You knew what to do."

Jack's mind had been in a whirlwind. Now he paused as well, and thought.

"I didn't plan it," he said. "It just sort of came out. It was a bit like Dunvik, wasn't it? Gosol worked like a charm."

"Not a charm, Jack, you know that. The power to fight evil," said Grandpa Sandy kindly. "But with Tamlina dead we've lost a powerful ally, and we've found an even more powerful enemy. I don't think Keldy is safe. We must get back to the castle."

"But are you all right, Grandpa?" Rana indicated her grandfather's right leg, which still smouldered. "What did Malevola use on you?"

"A curse unknown to me," admitted her grandfather, wincing in pain. "I need Armina. She may know how to heal these wounds."

Painfully, and painfully slowly, they moved cautiously through the woods back to Ossian's house. Stopping only to wash their hands there and collect their belongings, they set off for the low road.

8

The Phosphan Curse

The low road journey back was painful. Grandpa Sandy, barely able to stand, leant heavily on his grandsons' shoulders. Jack gritted his teeth, but still felt that his shoulder would break under the weight. The acrid smell from Grandpa's wounds was making Lizzie's travel sickness worse, and by the time they emerged at the foot of the castle square, they were all feeling wretched. They were met at the house by a fretful Aunt Katie, who clasped a handkerchief to her mouth as she saw her father-in-law.

"Quick, Rana," she said after a moment. "Go and get Armina. Boys, get Grandpa into the front room."

Armina arrived, sniffed a couple of times and quickly demanded a bowl of hawthorn oil and some clean cloths. "It's a Phosphan curse," she announced. "The burn has gone deep. I wish you'd got him to me sooner."

Jack opened his mouth to explain, but was silenced by a

look from Ossian. Jack left at Armina's request to go and find his uncle, and Gilmore the tailor.

How come we get the blame for things? he fumed. *We got him here as fast as we could.*

The news had spread quickly. Within minutes neighbours and friends were gathering in the square, wanting to know if they could help. Armina took control, sending some out for supplies of cure-stones and jyoti paste, ordering more cloths and arranging for sandalwood scrapings to be burnt. When she decided that Grandpa was fit to be moved, she organised a litter party, and together they carried Grandpa to her house, at the top of the square. Here, as Armina explained, she could look after his wounds. But − and she made this abundantly clear − the recovery was going to take time. Phosphan curses were notoriously difficult to treat, especially when they had had a chance to burn so deeply.

Jack and the others walked dejectedly home. When they got back, they met Petros, Uncle Hart and Aunt Dorcas, who had been out in the city and had missed all the commotion. Once Ossian had brought them up to date, Uncle Hart announced that they would have to go back to Keldy. There was no way he was leaving his home unattended if Malevola was around in the woods. Rejecting Aunt Katie's suggestion that it would be safer to send grigs to find out what was happening, Uncle Hart got his family organised and soon they were heading down to the low road.

"But what if those creatures are still there?" Lizzie couldn't help feeling that Keldy was still too dangerous. "And what were they, anyway?"

"The demon was like the ones at Dunvik," pointed out Jack.

"And the old man was a Dunter," explained Ossian. "You know, a Red Cap."

"Grandpa told me about them last year," said Jack thoughtfully. "They dip their caps in the victim's blood. But he said they came from the border lands. If Malevola came from one of the north islands, maybe the Unseelie are joining up from all over."

It was three days before Armina would let Grandpa Sandy have any visitors. Requests to see him were met with the blunt assertion that he wasn't well enough. When Jack and his cousins were finally allowed to enter Armina's house, it was under strict instructions not to touch anything.

As they passed into the hallway, Jack's nostrils were assaulted by an assortment of odours. The sandalwood he recognised, but there were other, more pungent aromas. Lizzie wrinkled her nose as Rana cautiously pushed open the door to the darkened room where their grandfather lay. A fire was crackling in the grate, but it threw little light into the room.

"Can we have a light on, please?" asked Rana timidly.

Tutting, Armina stuck her sceptre in a holder by the fire.

"Bright light is bad for his wounds. But moonlight is safe. *Lunalumen!*"

The sceptre glowed and the room looked as if bright moonlight was flooding in. Now they could make out their grandfather, lying on a couch.

"Five minutes only!" barked Armina. "He must rest!"

With that she withdrew, and the youngsters shuffled

awkwardly forward. Rana took hold of her grandfather's hand. His eyes opened, but for a moment he appeared not to see her. Then recognition dawned, and he smiled. Patting her hand, he mumbled inaudibly. For once, Rana was unable to speak. Tears welled up in her eyes.

"Are you all right, Grandpa?" whispered Lizzie.

He nodded, a slight movement that seemed to take from him what little energy he had. His eyes closed again, and he gave a gentle sigh.

Jack looked around the room nervously. His grandfather's wounds smelt disgusting. Armina entered and moved swiftly over to the fire, throwing a handful of wood scrapings onto the flames. There was a hiss and crackle of sparks as the scented wood met the blaze.

"The sandalwood cleans the air," she said matter-of-factly. "Now, Sandy, can you speak?"

Grandpa Sandy's eyes opened again, and he looked over to Jack. With an effort, he cleared his throat.

"Good boy."

Jack flushed, and blinked furiously to get rid of tears in the corner of his eyes.

"You stepped in again," continued Grandpa, his voice a little stronger. "You used Gosol. Never doubt its power, Jack. It's banished demons twice."

Jack moved over to his grandfather.

"You seemed all right up in Keldy. I thought you were just a bit wounded."

"It's the way Phosphan curses work, boy," stated Armina. "They burn slowly; at first the damage looks slight. That's why they must be treated quickly, before they burn down to the bone. I can heal it, but it will take many weeks. And now your grandfather must rest. You can see him again in a few days."

The four youngsters made their way outside.

"Poor Grandpa," reflected Rana. "I thought he was all right. That Malevola's an evil hag."

"Good job you got rid of her, then," stated Petros, punching Jack lightly on the shoulder.

"I don't know," said Jack. "I don't think she's gone for good somehow. She took something from Tamlina: did she still have her ring on?"

"I never noticed," admitted Rana.

"I didn't think Grandpa would be so badly hurt. What are we going to do without him?" asked Lizzie.

"What did Tamlina say, before she died?" demanded Rana. "Something about a cave, and a saint. Who could help us find out about that?

"There was a bridge too," stated Jack. "'The giant's bridge,' she said. And waking columns."

"It was to do with the Sphere, wasn't it?" Lizzie spoke up now. "Tamlina said that Malevola's come because she wants the Sphere. And something about the Kildashie."

There was a pause for a few moments.

"I know you won't like this," said Rana slowly, "but if it's Shian lore, your best bet is Murkle."

"Anything's better than asking him," blurted Petros. "He's torture."

"There were manuscripts too," asserted Jack. "I remember Grandpa talking about them last year. The ones Matthew left in the Stone Room."

"Matthew the Enchanter?" asked Lizzie.

"He wasn't an enchanter; at least, I don't think he was. He taught about Gosol. Anyway, he said he'd left some manuscripts in the Stone Room. Then Fenrig stole them and gave them to his dad. Maybe we should look for them first. Murkle's too much trouble."

"Honestly, boys." Rana spoke to her sister, her tone openly scornful. "They'd rather wander around in circles than ask for help."

"All right, if you're so smart, you go and ask him." Jack threw down the gauntlet. "I bet you don't get anywhere."

Rana and Lizzie looked at each other, then back at Jack. Both nodded.

"What d'you bet us?" demanded Rana.

"A silver sovereign," stated Petros. "But you've got to get chapter and verse from him. Everything: where the Sphere is, where the cave is . . ."

"And the bridge," butted in Jack.

"Nobody knows where the Sphere is, dimwit," said Lizzie. "Don't you think the Congress would have got it by now if Murkle knew where it was? But we'll get everything else. Agreed?"

The four shook hands on the deal.

As Lizzie and Rana headed for the house, Jack whispered urgently, "We need to find out before they do. Let's ask Daid. He must know something, especially if the Sphere is mixed up with the humans, like the Chalice was."

"Daid's being 'looked after', remember? We'll never get past Murkle."

"You'll have to distract him," said Jack. "Ask him about one of his stories. Or about how the Kildashie control sound. You get him out of the way, and I'll speak to Daid."

Petros had little enthusiasm for tackling Murkle on his own. "We'll both ask him," he said. "Maybe we can get them apart for a minute or two."

Jack couldn't think of a better plan, so the two made their way along to Murkle's house. For a while Jack's knock brought no answer; then they heard the sound of a bolt being drawn back.

"Who is it? What do you want?"

"It's Jack and Petros. Can we come in?"

There was a pause while Murkle appeared to weigh up this request. Then the door was pulled open, and Murkle ushered the youngsters into the front room. Daid sat on one of the chairs. He looked like he hadn't shaved for several days, his hair was unbrushed and his clothes seemed to hang off him.

"Sit down." Murkle's voice was flat.

Jack looked unsurely at Petros as they sat down.

"We . . . we wanted to ask you about how the Kildashie controlled the Blue Hag's echo. Someone said they had a silencer charm."

"The Tassitus?" snorted Murkle. "Impossible. It's not been heard of for centuries."

"But I was there when they did it," persisted Jack.

"Nonsense. A trick of the wind."

Jack looked awkwardly at Petros. This wasn't going very well.

"We also wondered about the giant who . . . who lived in the cave of the wells," stammered Jack.

Murkle's eyebrows shot up in surprise. This was a first for

him. His countenance brightened, and he moved swiftly to take his own chair. With barely a pause, he launched into the story, which Jack and Petros knew only too well. In desperation, Jack looked across at his cousin, but Petros appeared frozen to the spot. He stared blankly at some indeterminate point on the far wall.

"The Nebula giant has been asleep for countless centuries. He must be woken gently, and with a quartz stone with a double crescent moon . . ."

No respite. The minutes ticked by.

"And some giants can swim huge distances . . ."

The voice droned on and on.

"Even stone structures in some giants' caves can be made to waken by the simple hex 'Disuscito' – when the moon's full, of course . . ."

No respite.

After a few minutes, Jack realised he would have to take the initiative.

"Excuse me, Murkle, but could I go and get a drink, please? Daid can show me where things are."

Murkle frowned: he was not used to being interrupted. With a scowl, he waved Jack away and continued his recitation.

Jack stood up and went over to where Daid was sitting. Daid looked at him distractedly.

"Can you show me where the cups are, please?" Jack tried to keep his voice steady.

Daid appeared flustered, but he stood up and followed Jack to the kitchen. Walking across the dingy room, he indicated a cupboard. Jack screwed up his nose at the dank smell, but determined to pursue his goal.

"I wanted . . ." His voice faltered. "To ask you . . . about the papers Fenrig stole."

"You know, don't you?" Daid looked haunted as he spoke. "I don't know if it's the Stone, or the Kildashie. Oh, it's all terrible." He paced up and down, pausing only to grip the back of a chair. His fingernails dug deep into the wood, leaving scratch marks. "I should have taken them to the Congress, I know. But I'm not sure . . . some of them seem to want the Kildashie here."

"I don't know what . . ." began Jack, but then stopped. "When you said it might be the Stone or the Kildashie, what did you mean?"

Daid looked sadly at him. "Ever since Oestre, I've been unsure. I touched the Stone. The first Shian in hundreds of years. But I don't know if it happened because of Oestre or because the Kildashie did something. They're dangerous. The manuscripts may be lethal in the wrong hands, and the Congress is divided."

"Daid, d'you mean you've got the papers?" said Jack calmly.

Daid looked over at Jack and nodded sadly.

"I found them a few days after I'd touched the Stone. They were in a drawer I know I'd searched before. I don't know how I missed them."

Daid pulled a sheaf of tattered old parchments from inside his cardigan and placed them on the table. Jack immediately examined them. The writing on the fragile parchments was old-fashioned and very faint.

"Fenrig stole them, like you said, and he gave them to his father. But he stole them back again and left them here by mistake. Not a very bright boy." Daid's voice was flat.

"Do they say where the Sphere is?" asked Jack softly.

Daid shook his head.

"Do they talk of a saint's cave, or a bridge?" Jack persisted.

Daid's face momentarily lit up. "You know of the cave?" His eyes were eager, sparkling.

Jack paused. "We . . . we were told that the Sphere might be found where the cave is. Or at least that we must find the cave first."

Daid slumped into a chair. "The papers talk of a cave, but it's confusing. There's an ancient prophecy in the manuscripts, when children will cross a bridge from the cave and rescue a dead man."

Jack looked quizzically at Daid. He sensed that there was something else.

"What more do the papers say?" he urged.

Daid was silent. He hung his head; then, taking a deep breath, he looked Jack in the eye.

"They give the dead man a name."

There was an expectant pause, while Jack waited for Daid to continue.

The silence continued.

"And?" demanded Jack, his patience breaking.

"His name . . . is Phineas."

9

Secrecy and Trust

Jack's astonishment was interrupted immediately by the appearance of Murkle.

"What's going on? Why are you taking so long?" he demanded.

Daid sat slumped in his chair. Jack, suddenly giddy, had to grab another chair to stop himself from falling. Murkle looked quizzically from one to the other, while Petros peered in uncertainly from the doorway.

Then Murkle spotted the sheaf of papers on the table, and he stepped forward to examine them. Instinctively, Jack tried to grab them, but Murkle's hand was swifter.

"I'll take these." His voice was authoritative. "I think it's time we had a chat with Petros' father about this." He scooped up the manuscripts and, with a stern look at Daid, marched out of the kitchen.

"Why didn't you keep him in the front room?" hissed Jack as he moved to follow.

"I tried. You were taking too long," retorted Petros unapologetically.

Murkle had already left the house, and he turned and waved the youngsters on impatiently. With a sense of foreboding, Jack and Petros followed their tutor.

Uncle Doonya was standing in the doorway as the three of them approached the house. Murkle strode up and barked, "I want to know why you can't keep these impertinent young boys in line."

"Would you like to come in, Murkle? I think we can discuss this where the rest of the square cannot hear us." Uncle Doonya's voice was calm.

To Jack's surprise, Rana and Lizzie were already in the front room when they entered.

"These young boys came to my house under the false pretext of finding out about Shian folklore," began Murkle. "By some means, this one –" he indicated Jack "– tricked Daid into showing him these manuscripts."

"I didn't trick him, he just showed me them." Jack's tone was plaintive, but Uncle Doonya just held up his hand.

"I want to know why you allow these rascals to behave in such an underhand manner,' said Murkle. 'I showed them my hospitality, and they abused it."

"What hospitality?" demanded Petros. "You let us in, that's all. Jack had to ask for a drink."

"Shouting will get us nowhere." Uncle Doonya's voice was calm. "If the boys have upset your sense of hospitality, then I'm certain they will apologise." He looked commandingly at

Petros, then at Jack. "But I am sure that the Congress would be interested to know that you have these manuscripts. As you know, they were presumed missing."

Murkle looked uncertain for the first time. Then a look of steel came into his eyes.

"The Congress appears not to know which way to turn," he said icily. "These papers need to be deciphered properly, not shared with anyone who asks to see them."

"Be that as it may, Petros and Jack have done nothing wrong. If Daid was foolish enough to show Jack the papers, that is your responsibility. Daid is under your care, after all."

With a snort, Murkle stood up and marched out.

Uncle Doonya moved to the doorway and called Aunt Katie from the kitchen. Whispering to her, he left. Aunt Katie came in and closed the door behind her.

"You're all to stay here while your father has a word with Murkle." Then, seeing Jack's raised eyebrow, she added half-apologetically, "Oh, you know who I mean, Jack."

"Why d'you tell Dad where we'd gone?" Petros turned on Rana.

"That's enough!" snapped Aunt Katie. "Your father will be back soon."

Uncle Doonya returned just a couple of minutes later. He stood in the doorway, and for a few moments there was an awkward silence.

"You boys have got off very lightly," he said sternly. "Murkle's heart is in the right place, but he is a dangerous Shian to cross."

Uncle Doonya sat down now, and his tone was gentler.

"We're all upset because Grandpa's ill, but that's all the more reason to keep our heads."

"We already know some things," stated Jack. "What Tamlina told us, about the cave and the bridge. We were going to ask Daid for his help in finding out more."

"We wanted to know about the Sphere, Dad." Petros spoke up. "And about what happened to Grandpa, so maybe we could help."

"There's nothing wrong with wanting to help Grandpa. But it's hard to know who we can trust. Many of the Kildashie are wild, and although it pains me to say this, some of the Congress may not be relied upon."

"Is Murkle reliable, then?" asked Jack. His tone was just below impertinent, and for a moment Uncle Doonya looked angry. Then he smiled.

"Murkle's always been a bit fierce, even when I was an apprentice. But I've persuaded him to let me see the manuscripts. Now that he knows I know about them, it would be hard for him to say no. However, we must be careful about who else knows this – so it goes no further, all right?"

All of the youngsters indicated assent.

"It seems the manuscripts are a mixture. Murkle thought he could work out the Shian bits and Daid would take the human parts."

"Daid talked about a prophecy," said Jack uncertainly. "He said children would rescue a dead man called Phineas."

Aunt Katie let out a gasp, before recovering.

"Prophecies aren't always what they seem," she announced. "People find in them what they want. My father taught me that. And if it's Daid who's deciphering them, then they probably refer to humans."

Uncle Doonya looked down at the youngsters. "We need to get the right Shian in to examine these papers. That will give us the best chance."

"Why don't we ask Cosmo?" suggested Jack. "He knew a lot about the King's Chalice."

"And what about the ghosts?" asked Lizzie. "Comgall and his monks?"

"We called on them because they made the Chalice," pointed out Jack. "Why would they know about the Sphere?"

"Asking Cosmo might be what we need," said Uncle Doonya. "He certainly knew more than we realised."

"And he deliberately didn't tell the Congress," said Petros. Seeing his father's grim look, Petros persevered. "It's true, Dad. When the Congress summoned him in, he didn't tell them because he didn't trust all of them. And he was right: Rowan was a traitor."

Uncle Doonya sat down and cupped his face with his hands. When he spoke, he sounded weary.

"You're right. It's hard to accept that the Congress couldn't – can't – be trusted. The way some of them are willing to let the Kildashie stay is worrying. We'll have to do what we can without them for now." He turned to Jack. "Jack, you got on with Cosmo: can you ask him to come and see us, and we'll try to decipher the manuscripts?"

Jack nodded.

"Purdy knows some of the Cos-Howe boys," piped up Rana. "We can ask her to speak to them."

"It would be better coming from Jack. Petros can go along

too." Uncle Doonya's voice had regained its authority. "The low road can take you straight there. Anyone can use it now; no time like the present."

Jack looked across at Petros, who just stared back.

"When will Murkle let us have the papers?"

"Just find out when Cosmo can come here, and I'll deal with Murkle," replied Uncle Doonya. "I doubt he'll allow the manuscripts to leave the square."

Jack stood up and moved through to the front door. Petros remained in his chair for a few moments, then rose slowly and followed.

"You don't have to come," said Jack. "I can go and ask Cosmo myself."

Petros threw him a scornful look. "Dad said I've got to go with you."

"Suit yourself." Jack made his way down to the mound of earth behind the last house at the foot of the square. Petros followed on, dragging his steps a little. When he arrived at the mound he gripped Jack's arm and blurted out, "Wind-flock Cos-Howe."

It was an hour before Jack and Petros returned. As they entered the house, Rana's face emerged from the front room.

"'D'you find him?'" she asked breathlessly. Behind her, Lizzie and Aunt Katie looked anxiously on. Uncle Doonya wasn't present.

Petros pushed past Rana and sat down. Jack stood in the doorway.

"Sure, we found Cosmo," said Petros casually. "He said he'd be over later."

"Did you say why we wanted him?" asked Aunt Katie anxiously.

"Well, we had to," said Petros. "Otherwise why would he come?"

"Is he coming, then?" Uncle Doonya had reappeared, and his voice betrayed his fear that the quest had been fruitless.

"It's OK," said Jack. "I told him we had the manuscripts, and he could hardly wait. He said Oobit and Gandie had to come too. He wasn't sure if he'd be welcome here."

"Why ever not?" asked Aunt Katie innocently. "We all thought what he did at Dunvik was marvellous."

"He thinks Atholmor didn't like him taking control. He's not convinced that his followers would take kindly to him coming here."

Aunt Katie looked blank. "We don't follow Atholmor," she said simply. "He convenes the Congress, that's all."

"Whatever, Mum," said Petros wearily. "He just wasn't sure that coming here on his own was a good idea."

"The Congress represents all Shian in this part of the country," said Uncle Doonya emphatically. "If Cosmo can help to decipher these papers then he must help. I'll go and speak to Murkle."

Uncle Doonya returned fifteen minutes later with both Murkle and Daid. While Murkle looked stern, Daid was obviously anxious, and he wrung his hands together. As he entered, Uncle Doonya gave a "What could I do?" look to Aunt Katie. Taking his cue, Aunt Katie stood up and announced that she would prepare some refreshments for later.

"Rana, Lizzie, you come and give me a hand. Boys, you come through as well. I've got some errands for you to run."

"What d'you mean?" asked Petros indignantly. "We want to stay and read the papers with the others."

"Whippersnappers," muttered Murkle.

Jack stood up briskly. "Come on, Petros; we'll help the others out."

Petros looked blank for a moment. "Oh, all right. I mean, yes, of course."

"Come on," said Jack as Petros emerged from the front room. "They just want us out of the way. But I've got an idea."

As they reached the top of the stairs, Jack turned left to go into the girls' bedroom. Petros looked downstairs cautiously.

"What're you doing?" he demanded. "Rana'll go spare if she finds you in there. You know what she's like."

"Yes, I know," said Jack simply. "She's an eavesdropping telltale who wants to know everything that's going on but can't keep a secret."

"Fair enough," muttered Petros as he followed Jack cautiously into his sisters' room. "What're you looking for?"

"This," said Jack proudly, as he held up the beetler bonnet given to Rana and Lizzie the previous autumn.

"The beetler!" said Petros breathlessly. "Oh, wait a minute, I'm not putting that on again. I nearly got killed wearing that; it gives me the heebie-jeebies."

"Don't worry, I'll wear it," said Jack patiently. "As soon as Cosmo and the others get here, they'll start with the manuscripts, right? I'll go into the front room and listen in."

"So what d'you want me to do?" said Petros.

"Just keep the others out of the way. I don't want people

tramping in and out of the room; they might step on me. Just make sure they all stay in the kitchen, or out of the house altogether. OK?"

"All right. I'll say you've gone up to see Lee-Brog or someone. That way Mum won't be looking for you."

The Cos-Howe "crew", as Jack thought of them, arrived a couple of hours later. Uncle Doonya, Murkle and Daid were in the front room poring over the manuscripts, which they had spread over the floor. Civilities were exchanged and the business in hand explained. Having brought in the refreshments, Aunt Katie, Rana, Lizzie and Petros withdrew to the kitchen, and the work in the front room began in earnest.

Jack crept down the stairs and noted that the kitchen door was shut. In his hand he clutched the silk cap made by Freya. It was so fine he could hardly feel the cloth at all. Inwardly, he marvelled at her tailoring skills. *Oh well,* he thought, *here we go.* Checking again that all the doors off the hallway were closed, he put the cap on his head. Immediately, Jack shrank to the size of a beetle.

10
The Beetler Cap

Whoaah! Weird!

Jack was well used to the growing and shrinking as he went in and out of the Shian gate to the human spaces, and to the "squeezing up" as they were made to shrink to fit into Murkle's front room for lessons, but this was something else altogether. Jack had never felt so tiny, so vulnerable, in his life.

He tried hard to remember what Rana had said about using the beetler when she had listened in to the Congress discussions in the same front room the year before. There was something you had to avoid: but what? Jack had just got to the base of the door when he became aware of movement to his left. He froze, and looked over. There it was again, at the very base of the door hinge: an enormous spider. Jack hurriedly moved in the opposite direction and passed under the door.

This room is gigantic, he thought, as he looked up at the

ceiling. Everything seemed so far away and so high up. He was aware of voices, but found the sounds hard to make out: a bit echoey. Were they arguing? After a moment or two his ears tuned in to the sounds, and he realised that it was just more than one person talking at the same time. *The skirting board*, he thought, *that's where Rana said she hid*. He scurried over to the side of the room and settled down to listen.

"What else can it possibly mean?" demanded Murkle angrily. "The paper quite clearly talks about a saint's cave."

"Have you any idea how many saints there are?" replied Cosmo heatedly. "And how many caves are linked to saints? The humans have wandered about for centuries naming places, often without any real idea of why. It would be like – how do they put it? – looking for a needle in a haystack."

"Most of these papers are of human origin," said Daid quietly. "I do have some understanding of how they think."

"Then explain to us, please, what this bit here means." Murkle sounded annoyed.

"It's complicated; these parchments are very old, and the script is not of our age." Daid's voice was weary. "It will take time to read them and put them together in the right order. We don't even know if this is the full set."

"Well, let me look at the Shian papers then," demanded Murkle. "It is my area of expertise, after all."

"But the whole point is that they're together, don't you see that?" Cosmo tried to keep the heat out of his voice. "We can't look at one part without the other."

"Then for goodness' sake let us decide on a strategy, otherwise we will get nowhere," snapped Murkle. "I propose that we meet each evening to read and discuss."

"There are dozens of parchments," pointed out Uncle Doonya. "That will take weeks."

"Then let's make an inventory of what we have and divide up the work," said Cosmo. It was more a command than a suggestion. Taken aback by his tone, Murkle muttered under his breath something about knowing your place, but he found he could not disagree.

An hour later they had sifted through most of the parchments and were beginning to put them into piles. Jack was getting bored. He had hoped to catch some vital information, but it looked like they were a long way off getting that far. Warily, he moved back under the door, taking care to note that the spider had not moved. Once he was back in the hallway he reached up and dislodged the cap from his head. In a second he had regained his normal height, but as he stood up . . .

"*Oww!*" screeched Rana, and she thumped Jack on the side of the head.

As Jack stumbled he felt the beetler cap catch on the edge of a shelf. He quickly pushed the cap down into his pocket.

Aunt Katie came running out of the kitchen. "Honestly, I can't let you out of my sight for a minute."

Rana glowered at Jack as they trudged into the kitchen. Jack tried to indicate that she should shut up, but Rana's back was up.

"He stood on my foot, Mum," she claimed loudly.

"Rana . . ." Jack's voice was hushed, but urgent.

Luckily, Aunt Katie appeared not to notice anything untoward, and she admonished both. There was a moment's silence. "How's Lee-Brog, then, dear?" enquired Aunt Katie of Jack.

"Oh, er ... fine. He wasn't in. I mean, we went up to the High Street, er ... for a walk." Jack stuttered through the first excuse he could think of. His aunt had started to wash some vegetables at the kitchen sink and was only half listening.

"That's good, dear," she said absent-mindedly. "Now, where did I put those ash berries? I need to rinse them ..."

Jack took the opportunity of his aunt's preoccupation to slip out of the kitchen. He stole upstairs and quickly replaced the beetler cap in Rana's drawer. Coming back downstairs, he found that Cosmo and the others were just leaving.

"How're you getting on?" he asked, as innocently as he could.

"Murkle doesn't want to let the manuscripts out of his sight," admitted Uncle Doonya. "But we've made some progress." His voice tried to sound cheerful, but it was less than convincing.

"Is it going to take ages then?" asked Rana.

"We'll have to see," was all her father would say.

Depressingly, that set the tone for the next two weeks. Each evening Murkle would bring the manuscripts around, Daid following sombrely behind him. Cosmo and the others appeared from the low road entrance, and together with Uncle Doonya, they would shut themselves in the front room and pore over the papers. They gave little away as they broke up a couple of hours later.

The lack of urgency partly reflected the news from Keldy. Malevola had not been heard of since her encounter with Jack, and life — according to Uncle Hart — had returned to normal. Closer to Edinburgh, the Kildashie were posing no obvious threat either. They kept themselves to themselves in their camp just outside the city. All in all, the task of deciphering the manuscripts seemed to become less urgent.

Nevertheless, Jack was restless: like the others, he wanted to find the cave and the bridge, but he especially wanted to know if the Phineas in the prophecy was his father. Jack had considered using the beetler cap again, but to his annoyance found that Rana's suspicions had led her to tidy her things away more carefully. On asking her where the cap was, she had simply repeated that what was hers was hers, and he could go whistle.

Jack's frustration at the slow progress with the manuscripts was mirrored by his grandfather's tediously slow recovery. The youngsters could visit most days now, but Grandpa Sandy remained weak, and the acrid smell from his wounds made the visits less than pleasant. Jack and the others would come away from Armina's house glad to get some fresh air again.

"Poor Grandpa," said Lizzie for the umpteenth time after one such visit. "I wish we could do something for him."

"Is Armina making him any better?" asked Petros. It wasn't an accusation, more a casual enquiry.

"There's no one else knows how to heal wounds like he's got," stated Rana emphatically. "And anyway, he trusts her."

"D'you think he's told her what Tamlina said?" wondered Rana.

"Shouldn't think so," replied Jack. "He probably can't remember much except the pain."

"He wasn't so bad to start with," pointed out Rana. "Before the Phosphan burnt deep he asked her questions."

Jack thought back to the time they had been in the woods at Keldy. Rana was right. Their grandfather *had* been clear-headed to begin with, but since getting back he'd been so weak. It was inconceivable that he could have been having detailed discussions with Armina.

Jack decided that it was time to use the beetler again, but he knew that he would have to persuade Rana and Lizzie. He tried an indirect approach.

"I bet we know more than you do about the manuscripts."

"Oh yes?" replied Rana scornfully. "All you've found out is that children will cross a bridge and rescue a dead man."

"Called Phineas," pointed out Jack. "You think that's coincidence? Anyway, we had a bet. But we'll forget about the money if you'll share the beetler with us. That way we can listen in."

"What makes you think the beetler will work?" demanded Rana.

"You used it last year. Why can't we use it again?"

"Because you tore it, and Freya can't get the silk thread she needs to mend it."

"All right, but when you get it back we can all use it. And we'll call it quits over the bet."

However, it was more than a week before Freya obtained the necessary thread, and news about the manuscripts was rare. None of those poring over the papers was inclined to share their findings – if indeed they had any to share.

Once Freya had finally presented Rana and Lizzie with the mended beetler, it was decided that Jack would get to use the cap again, because the name Phineas had been linked with the manuscripts, and he probably had most to gain.

That evening, when the Cos-Howe crew arrived, Jack and the others were all in the kitchen. As ever, they made a point of greeting the visitors, in the hope that they would be asked to join in. But, as usual, Cosmo and the others quickly secreted themselves in the front room with Uncle Doonya, Murkle and Daid.

"We'll give them twenty minutes," said Jack. "The speed they're going, we won't miss much."

However, even this short time proved too long for their patience. After fifteen minutes, Rana and Lizzie distracted their mother in the kitchen while Jack went out to the hallway. As he had done before, he gently placed the beetler cap on his head. The shrinking sensation was no less strange, but Jack quickly scuttled towards the base of the front room door. The spider wasn't there, thank goodness; he could do without that. Once inside the room, Jack took up the same position by the side wall.

It took a minute or two for him to tune in to the voices again. They weren't arguing this time. If anything, they seemed excited.

"The clue's in the overlap." It was Daid who was talking. "These Shian manuscripts talk of the giant's bridge, and these human papers mention the saint's cave. But this one here is the only parchment that mentions both, and it talks of the Sphere. For the humans it's a flag map, but for Shian it's a globe that shows your true path. It's the third treasure."

"This torn bit even gives the cave a name – or part of it: Fin-something," said Cosmo emphatically. "But this bit here isn't human, it's Low Elvish; it describes the bridge, and a Taniwah in the pit of torment at the end."

Murkle grabbed the frail parchment, causing Uncle Doonya to exclaim, "Careful! That's hundreds of years old!"

Murkle examined sections of it minutely, then silently put the manuscript down. "It *is* mixed," he conceded. "It's the first time I've heard of something that was both Shian and human."

"The pit of torment must be significant," said Cosmo. "What do we know about Taniwah lizards?"

"Their gaze is fatal, but they are powerless in sunlight or moonlight," snapped Murkle. "Any fool knows that."

"The Sphere is the real prize," stated Daid firmly. "Whoever has that will be powerful, especially if he can put it together with the Stone and the Chalice."

"So now we need to find St Fin-whatever's cave," stated Oobit.

Jack heard no more. He was suddenly conscious of something moving to his right. Looking round, he saw to his horror that a huge spider was advancing slowly towards him. Panicking, he reached up and grabbed the beetler cap that perched on top of his head. Instantly, he grew to his normal size.

Jack was briefly aware of a shocked silence in the room. Six sets of eyes turned towards him. Instinctively, he made a dash for the door, but Murkle's hand shot out. Jack yelped in pain as a ragged, grimy fingernail scraped across the back of his left hand. Blood welled up instantly.

Murkle had moved swiftly forward; he reached out again, and this time he made no mistake, gripping Jack firmly by the collar.

"Gotcha!"

11

Household Chores

Jack nearly lost his nerve. Murkle's grip on him was fierce, and although his first impulse had been to try to squirm free, he realised that this would do no good. Looking calmly up at Murkle's triumphant features, he said quietly, "Are we going to St Fin's cave, then?"

Murkle exploded.

"Why, you young . . ." But as he made to swipe Jack with his free hand, Uncle Doonya stepped in.

"That's enough, Murkle. Let's see what Jack has to say for himself."

Murkle relaxed his grip, but did not let go altogether. Uncle Doonya spoke again.

"Jack, you owe us an explanation."

"You're trying to find out about my father," said Jack simply. "I've a right to know what you know." He looked at his uncle, who stared fixedly back.

Alerted by Murkle's shout, Aunt Katie now burst in. "Whatever's happened?" she exclaimed. Then, seeing Jack, she stopped abruptly. "Jack, what on earth are you doing here?"

"This impertinent pup has been hiding in here," snapped Murkle. "If others were to find out that he knows something . . ." His voice trailed off.

"Murkle's right, Jack." Cosmo stepped forward. "You're putting yourself in danger."

"I've a right . . ." started Jack, but he got no further. A shout from Aunt Katie surprised everyone.

"Your hand! It's bleeding!"

To an outraged gasp from Murkle, she dragged Jack away to the kitchen, where she deftly wrapped a linen bandage around the hand.

Rana and Lizzie watched in silence, unsure how they could help. If they admitted knowledge of what he had been doing, would they end up in trouble too? Jack glanced over at them while his aunt bandaged his hand, but said nothing.

His hand throbbing, Jack was marched back to the living room to face the others. While he had been in the kitchen, they had clearly consulted about the most appropriate course of action. Uncle Doonya spoke.

"Jack, we appreciate that you want to find out about your father, but you must be patient. The information in these papers may be dangerous in the wrong hands. You're grounded for a fortnight, and for the next week you'll report to Murkle's house after supper to help clean it. After that we'll review matters."

"That's not fair . . . !" began Jack, but he was silenced by a ferocious bark from his uncle.

"Enough! Now, go to your room. We have been delayed too long already."

Jack found out the next day how bad things were. His morning in Gilmore's workshop was difficult: his left hand hurt badly and he found stitching almost impossible. He could feel his hand pulsing, each thud a reminder of his wound. The worst, however, was the treat in store for Jack after supper.

Murkle opened his front door and motioned for Jack to come in. Going through to the kitchen, Murkle pointed to a bucket and a pile of cloths.

"The wall around the stove needs cleaned," he said matter-of-factly.

Jack peered in the bucket of water and saw a bar of soap at the bottom.

"There's a room to do upstairs when you've finished that." Murkle turned and left.

Jack looked around. The dingy, cluttered kitchen was even grimier than he'd remembered. The stove showed signs of cooking, but not cleaning. Smears of fat and grease decorated the wall behind it. Beside the stove, several dirty pans were piled up on sauce-encrusted plates.

After thirty or forty minutes, Jack felt he had got as much grime off as he could. He looked with satisfaction at how dirty the water had become. Feeling pleased that he had done so well, Jack went to find Murkle.

His tutor was in the front room, reading, but there was no sign of Daid. Seeing Jack at the door, Murkle stood up and wordlessly followed him to the kitchen.

"You haven't done the dishes," snapped Murkle, turning round and going back to the front room.

Jack was speechless and briefly considered just walking out. Then, realising that he wouldn't get far unless Murkle was satisfied, he set to his task. Washing dishes with only one hand was harder than he'd realised, and Jack took some time to accomplish this. When he asked Murkle to come through and check that the task had been done, Murkle merely glanced at the stove and sink and muttered, "You can do the upstairs room tomorrow. Goodnight."

Jack trudged home, weary after his efforts, and dreading the thought of a whole week of housework in the dirtiest house he'd ever been inside.

When he got home, Aunt Katie asked how he'd got on.

"All right," he mumbled. "My hand's sore, though; I couldn't use it." He showed his bandaged hand to his aunt. Carefully, she peeled back the layers of the bandage and uttered a shriek of horror as she saw the mess underneath.

"It's infected!" she exclaimed. "Och, I should have cleaned it better."

She sat Jack down at the table and got to work with cleaning his wound. The edges were red and inflamed; a yellowy-green gunge oozed along the length of the cut.

"Well, there's no question of you going back to that filthy house," she stated. "The last thing you need is to get that wound any dirtier."

Jack smiled. There's always a silver lining.

"And stitching at Gilmore's was really difficult too," he announced, in the hope that he would have the whole day free to himself. His aunt looked at him sternly.

"I know what you're thinking, Jack. This is supposed to be a punishment. We'll see what your uncle says when he comes in."

She dusted some hyperox powder onto his hand and tied a fresh bandage around it. His hand still hurt, but the knowledge that he didn't have to go back and clean any more of Murkle's house was some compensation.

However, Jack's hopes of free days were dashed as soon as his uncle returned. It took Uncle Doonya only a few minutes to make alternative arrangements, and he announced with satisfaction that for the next week Jack would have day and evening lessons with Finbogie.

At Finbogie's house the next morning, Jack was subjected once again to a list of charms that had to be learnt. Laboriously, he tried to commit them to memory, but his painful hand and sense of grievance about his punishment combined to destroy his concentration.

When he returned that evening, Finbogie decided to test him on what he knew. Picking up *Morven's Book of Defence*, he started asking Jack questions.

"How do you defend yourself against a Taniwah?"

Jack wracked his brains. He knew he'd read something about Taniwahs, but for the life of him he couldn't recall what it was. Finbogie interpreted Jack's silence correctly and moved on.

"Well, what about a Ban-Finn?"

Casting about for possible connections, Jack could only come up with the name of one of the Congress members. "Er, is that like Ban-Eye?" said Jack nervously, recalling the bad-tempered old woman. He tried hard not to stare at Finbogie's scar.

"Well, they both have a connection to water, but that's not going to help you much, is it? All right, how about a Hobshee?"

Jack couldn't think of any answer.

"Well, you're not going to be much use defending yourself if you're attacked, are you?" Finbogie sounded more weary than angry.

"I used Gosol to banish Amadan last year. And it worked again with Malevola when she attacked Grandpa," Jack replied testily, but he had to admit to himself that he didn't really understand how Gosol worked. He knew it only worked when it *felt* right, and he couldn't just make that happen whenever he wanted. It was about really *believing* it, but he couldn't explain it, to himself or to Finbogie.

"I heard you used a sceptre on both occasions," said Finbogie quietly. "As you're not yet fourteen you're not supposed to use one."

"Would you rather I let Amadan and Malevola win, then?" demanded Jack.

"Of course not," snapped Finbogie, whose patience was clearly not endless. "But you might not always have access to a sceptre: what will you do then?"

Jack was stumped for an answer. He looked down, avoiding Finbogie's piercing stare.

"There are dangerous Shian around us, Jack. The Kildashie may be quiet at present, but they pose a very real threat. Some of them are barbarians. And you already know of many other dangerous creatures. You have to learn how to look after yourself." Finbogie paused, and his tone became easier. "You're a bright lad, Jack. But don't think you've nothing to learn. That's the surest way to end up dead."

Jack's eyes opened wide at the severity of this comment. He looked at Finbogie, trying to work out how to reply. Finbogie saved him the trouble.

"I'm going to teach you some basic techniques," said Finbogie. "But you can't do it without knowing *why* things work. You may think that learning charms and hexes is a waste of time, but one day it could save your life. Now, we'll start with the Dunters."

"You mean Red Caps? One threw his cap at Lizzie, and it was all covered in Tamlina's blood. Then he just vanished."

"So you don't know how he got away, then?"

Jack shook his head. Finbogie picked up *Morven's Book of Defence* again and leafed through until he came to a page about Dunters.

"There," he said, indicating a paragraph. "How to hex a Red Cap away. If you let him disappear, he can reappear whenever he wants."

Jack looked at the page. Sure enough, there was a hex that would have got rid of the Dunter up in Keldy.

"Absango." Jack mouthed the word.

"But you have to twist your right palm at him at the same time," explained Finbogie. "Just saying the word isn't enough. You have to show the Dunter what you're doing."

Jack felt a mixture of emotions. Finbogie's lessons had always been a form of torture, but that was because all they'd done was write out charms and try to learn hexes off by heart. This was explaining *why*; suddenly it started to make sense.

They practised the hex, using the wall as an imaginary Dunter. Jack soon learnt how to twist his hand and say the hex word at the right speed, and a small patch of the wall began to smoulder.

"That's enough for now," announced Finbogie after a while. "On Monday we'll continue with self-defence, then we'll start on how to recognise a shape-shifter. Many Shian have come to grief because they didn't know what to do with an evil shape-shifter. And Jack," continued Finbogie, "I wouldn't tell the other apprentices what you're doing just yet. I'll have to make arrangements if they're all going to learn practical hexes." He looked with a frown at the side wall, which smouldered slightly. "My house isn't designed for this."

Jack felt curiously pleased with himself as he went home. If he was going to learn real-life hexes and charms, maybe this punishment wasn't going to be so bad after all.

12

The Devil's Shoestring

Jack presented himself at Finbogie's house on Monday morning and was shown a series of demonstrations of self-defence. His confidence grew: he learnt how to disarm pucks, how to remain immune to the charms of a glastig and how to cast a hex that would stun any creature with a sword.

Negladius. He'd liked the sound of that one.

As Jack was led through each charm and hex, he felt his sore hand throb, a reminder of why he was there. It was a curious thing: his hand hurt like anything, and these lessons were a punishment, but he knew he was learning crucial skills. He was even starting to enjoy himself.

That evening, Jack's session with Finbogie moved up a gear.

"I'm going to teach you something that very few apprentices of your age will know," began Finbogie. "Living among humans all the time, there's nothing to test them — except the humans."

"You said something about shape-shifters," said Jack helpfully.

"You do get shape-shifters here. City Shian have adapted – they go for animals the humans expect to see. Dogs and cats mostly, foxes too, and birds are popular, especially blackbirds and ravens. We'll start with learning how creatures shape-shift," he continued. "What do you know about this?"

Jack thought. "My grandpa told me only some Shian can do this, and only at certain times."

"That's correct. You've had a good tutor there." Finbogie paused. "Terrible shame what happened to your grandfather."

Jack pondered this. It should be his grandfather teaching him now; he was happy to be learning, but he felt a bit guilty.

"This works best at the full moon," continued Finbogie. "Many shape-shifters transform themselves with a yucca hoop. What you need is yucca fibre, treated with oil and vinegar."

"You mean it's all wet?"

"Only up to a point. What do the vinegar and the oil do?"

Jack knew that the two didn't mix easily, but what this meant for plant fibres he couldn't imagine.

"The oil gets into the fibres – the vinegar keeps it there," pointed out Finbogie patiently. "But if they're near other yucca fibres, the oil oozes out. So to know if there's a shape-shifter around, carry a yucca loop."

"Is that all it is?" It didn't seem very complicated.

"Two other things you need to know," went on Finbogie. "Firstly, keep an eye out. Many shape-shifters use twelve sticks or knives arranged in a circle. If you ever see that, take care. And feel for the yucca in your pocket."

"But that doesn't teach me what to do about shape-shifters."

"In most cases, you get yourself out of there. This jomo bag charm works for most creatures, not just shape-shifters. You'd do well to keep it with you all the time. You must mix some dirt from three different places in the bag."

Finbogie pulled from his pocket a small red cloth bag.

"How'ds it work?" asked Jack. He had the feeling he'd seen a bag like that in Gilmore's workshop.

"The cloth is charmed," explained Finbogie. "The three dirts confuse your attacker and allow you to escape."

"You mean you don't deal with the shape-shifter?" Jack had expected to be taught how to disarm or overpower another creature. Running away didn't seem very brave. For the moment, he'd forgotten how useful the Aximon charm had been in escaping from Konan the previous year.

"Jack, until you're a lot older, you'll find that getting away safely is your best option. What you have to do is throw the mixed dirt at the feet of whoever – or whatever – is attacking you, and shout 'Asafetid'. But as you're so keen, we'll make a start on tackling certain creatures. Cats are usually easy; so are dogs, unless it's really fierce, then you have to stun it. Have you ever seen a stun hex?"

Jack thought back to his most recent trip to Keldy.

"Malevola used one against my cousin. But she used a sceptre."

"We're assuming that you won't have a sceptre," pointed out Finbogie. "What you need is something from the creature that's threatening you. Dogs are likely to be the fiercest, so we'll start with that."

"I can handle dogs," stated Jack. "My uncle Doonya taught

me how to calm a dog down with a 'Kynos' hex. But I've never trusted cats. They're revolting."

"We can cover both. You need to get hold of some strands of different animals' hair and braid them into a wristlet with one strand of silverweed. It's called a devil's shoestring. If you're threatened, put it on. It's like you tie the animal's legs together. Then use your jomo bag and get away."

It reminded Jack of something and he tried to concentrate. Suddenly his eyes blazed. "So it's like an Aximon, then? You just keep it in your pocket?"

Catching his drift, Finbogie said, "You can get weighed down carrying every charm you might ever need. That's where a Sintura belt comes in. It'll carry all sorts, and you'll not even know you're wearing it."

Striding over to a cupboard, Finbogie pulled open one of the doors. From a hanger he drew a dull green piece of cloth, which he cradled gently in both hands.

"Doesn't look like much, does it?" he asked with a look of satisfaction.

Jack inspected the cloth. It had several small pouches, and a buckle at one end. Deftly, Finbogie flicked the cloth, spinning one end around his waist. Tying the buckle, Jack was astonished to see the cloth disappear in front of his eyes.

"How'ds it do that?" he asked incredulously.

"I can see that Gilmore hasn't got round to teaching you about this, then," stated Finbogie. "Well, that's not surprising. They're expensive. The cloth comes from Ireland. But the stitching thread – that's a closely guarded secret. I've heard it's Japanese, or possibly Chinese. But I do know it works."

"So how can I get one?" Jack was filled with a new respect

for Gilmore, guessing correctly that he had made this belt for Finbogie.

"Well, you're working with Gilmore. I imagine that if you show aptitude and keenness, he may agree to make you one. For a fee."

Jack's heart sank. His lessons with Gilmore hadn't been going so well recently; he couldn't see the tailor doing him any favours. Seeing his disconsolate look, Finbogie went on, "Don't take it so hard. Just remember, if you're dealing with a shape-shifter, you need to get the wristlet — and one with all the common hairs. Animals — and people."

"You mean I just put the wristlet on?"

"You need to know what you're dealing with and say the right hex. For a cat it would be 'Felavert'. And remember, the same hex works for animals that are like cats. So use 'Felavert' for lynx and cougars as well. Any animal with a cleft foot it's 'Divisungulam.' For a dog it's 'Abcanidæ'."

As he drifted off to sleep that night, Jack rehearsed these hex names and thought about the ways in which he would defend himself if the need arose. The one problem he couldn't resolve was how to get hold of a Sintura belt. He was going to need one to keep all the various charms and wristlets he was starting to collect.

Jack had reason to start worrying about how to carry all his self-defence equipment. Over the next week Finbogie taught him several more charms and hexes to detect and ward off a whole host of shape-shifters, from ravens and seagulls to goats and bulls. Finbogie had embraced his new role as personal coach and teacher with an enthusiasm for which he was not famed. Only in these one-to-one sessions did Finbogie find that he could teach effectively, and his regular donations to Jack's collection meant Jack was forced to keep his charms and hexes in a box under his bed.

And more good news: Grandpa Sandy was finally on the mend. He would be fit enough to go home at the weekend, and could be seen taking short strolls in the square, always under Armina's watchful gaze.

Jack's poisoned hand was the only dampener. When he restarted his sessions in Gilmore's workshop, his hand was getting better, but it was still painful, and Jack found he couldn't achieve anything like the results he was trying for. At the back of his mind was the thought that he had to win Gilmore over if he wanted to ask for a Sintura belt. It was an added annoyance that Fenrig, to everyone's surprise, was starting to take his apprenticeship seriously. He turned up on time, was rarely insolent, and tidied up without complaint. Even the first session back with Daid – which started back that week – found the young Brashat polite and attentive. Fenrig's change of behaviour slightly unnerved Jack.

Maybe Fenrig's not so bad after all ... Jack mused as he wandered home from the workshop on Friday afternoon. *No, that's not true. Fenrig's concealing his true nature, that's all. He can't stay well behaved forever.* Jack smiled to himself. *Fenrig doesn't fool me.*

Then Jack saw him: a small, wizened old man near the foot of the square. And in his hands, a grubby red cap.

13
Return to Cos-Howe

Jack's heart raced. He blinked and stared hard. There was no doubt about it: it was the Dunter from the woods at Keldy. The old man watched Jack with wry amusement as the youngster froze on the spot. Then he held up his right forefinger so that Jack focussed on it, and with a slow and deliberate movement, drew the finger across his throat.

Jack gulped. There was no mistaking the meaning of the Dunter's action, but Jack had no time to respond, for the old man simply vanished. Jack hadn't even had time to think about the hex Finbogie had taught him.

He hurried back to the house, desperate to tell someone – anyone – what he had just seen. Running into the kitchen, he found his aunt kneading dough on the table. Flour was liberally dusted around the table, and Aunt Katie's hair was grey where the flour had wafted up.

"There's a Dunter in the square!"

Aunt Katie stopped and wiped a floury hand across her face.

"A Dunter? Here?" Her voice wavered.

"He was at the foot of the square. It was the one we saw in Keldy, I'm sure."

Hearing the commotion, Rana, Lizzie and Uncle Doonya entered the kitchen.

"Who did you see?" demanded Rana.

"The Dunter from Keldy. But he disappeared again."

"Are you sure it was him? It could have been another one."

Jack had to admit that he couldn't be absolutely sure. He had only ever seen one Dunter; maybe they all looked pretty much the same.

Uncle Doonya ran to the bottom end of the square, but there was no trace of the old man. Jack was left again with the uncomfortable knowledge that a deadly opponent was able to disappear at will.

At supper that night, the subject of apprentice safety was the main topic of conversation.

"If there are Dunters running around Edinburgh, I don't want any of you out in the city," proclaimed Aunt Katie.

"But we can't stay in the square all the time," protested Jack. "Anyway, the Dunter can get into the square; we're no safer here."

"I just don't like it," his aunt said. "They're horrible creatures. At least if you're here, I can keep an eye on you."

The youngsters exchanged surreptitious looks. There was no way they were going to be kept under the castle every day.

"We can't really keep them here all the time," said Uncle Doonya quietly to his wife.

"Especially this weekend," blurted Lizzie, excited about the forthcoming May Day festivities. "It's the Beltane party at Cos-Howe."

Aunt Katie's eyes were as round as saucers. "If you think I'm letting you lot out to Cos-Howe when there are bloodthirsty demons running around the city, you are all *very* much mistaken."

Uncle Doonya steered Aunt Katie out of the kitchen and into the front room. When they had gone, Rana snapped, "You shouldn't have told her about the party. We could've sneaked out and she wouldn't have known. Now she's going to be watching us like a hawk."

"We'll still get to the party," said Petros confidently. "Dad'll talk her round. You saw the way he took her out just now."

When Uncle Doonya and Aunt Katie returned to the kitchen, Aunt Katie avoided their gaze. Uncle Doonya spoke.

"As long as I come with you, you can go to the party at Cos-Howe. It can be an early treat for Jack's birthday. I'll keep an eye out for any Dunters."

"Er, actually, Dad, we haven't been invited yet," announced Petros, at which Rana gave him a swift kick under the table.

"What?" squeaked Aunt Katie. "Do you mean to say no one's invited you? Well, why on earth do you think you're going, then?" Her eyes blazed with indignation.

"Purdy and Freya are arranging it, Mum," said Rana. "It's how things are done."

"Well, it's not how things were done in my day. And the Cos-Howe Shian as well – well, some of them need taking in hand, that's all I'm going to say."

"You have to admit that they did a lot at Dunvik last year," pointed out Jack. "If it wasn't for Cosmo, we'd never have got the Chalice back. And they've been helping with the manuscripts."

"We're stuck with those," admitted Uncle Doonya. "We know about the cave and the ..." His voice trailed off as he saw the look in Aunt Katie's eyes. There was a silence for a few moments.

"I admit that Cosmo is a good young lad," stated Aunt Katie, pointedly ignoring what Uncle Doonya had been saying. "And his friends did help your grandfather, so I suppose they're not so bad. But you do hear terrible stories about what they get up to."

"You shouldn't believe half the stories you hear, Mum," stated Petros. "Dad'll be there, and Ossian too. We'll be all right."

It was agreed that the youngsters could go – providing they had a proper invitation – as long as Uncle Doonya was there to keep an eye on things. Petros gave Jack a knowing look as they made their way out to the square, as if to say, *He'll not be keeping an eye on me!*

Why hasn't Cosmo invited us anyway? pondered Jack as he made his way upstairs that night. Still, a Cos–Howe party was a better way to celebrate his thirteenth birthday than anything he might get at home. Dunter or no Dunter, he was going to Cos–Howe.

Grandpa Sandy returned home just before lunchtime the next day. He was pale and looked older, but the glint in his eyes showed that the fire inside was still there. However, when Lizzie asked how Malevola had managed to defeat him, she was scolded ferociously by her mother and spent the rest of the meal sobbing quietly.

"We're all going to the Beltane party tomorrow night," announced Petros, trying to raise the mood. "At Cos-Howe."

Grandpa Sandy smiled. "I'm sure you'll enjoy yourselves. Some good youngsters in Cos-Howe."

"I was saying yesterday how Cosmo and the others helped at Dunvik," stated Jack. "And Purdy's arranged for us to get invites."

Aunt Katie arched her eyebrows at this, but Rana confirmed, "Honestly, Mum. Purdy spoke with Gandie, and he said it's all right. And anyway, Dad's coming."

"Well, you just watch out for that Dunter," said Aunt Katie.

"It's all right, I'll keep an eye on them."

Uncle Doonya sounded confident, but Jack caught him looking quickly at Grandpa Sandy as he spoke. Although he really wanted to go to the party, a feeling deep inside Jack was telling him that something wasn't right.

However, late the next evening, Jack had to concede that his worries had been unfounded. The Cos-Howe party was everything he'd hoped for. Burning torches decked the great hall, the food was magnificent and the entertainment had been superb. The previous summer's party – Jack's first big party – had been tame by comparison. Several Irish Phooka had flown in and had performed a series of sketches and dances, a wild mixture of history, comedy and song. An old Lunanti Shee gave an expert display of baton twirling with his blackthorn stick, while a tall green-clad Fiannat sang songs of old battles. Korrigans were playing on instruments Jack didn't even recognise. The korrigans at Falabray the previous year had been timid and shy; these ones were playing music with expertise and real passion.

Jack wandered happily from one food-laden table to another. An hour later, and unable to eat any more, he sat down happily to watch the songs and dances on the various stages. It seemed bigger than he remembered, and he was embarrassed to be told scornfully by Petros that the whole place had been charmed for the night.

"It's Beltane," stated Petros, as he sat down beside Jack. "Didn't you realise they'd put on a special show? Everyone's having a good time – even the Kildashie are behaving themselves."

They both looked across to where a dozen Kildashie were grouped together, still not really joining in, but posing no threat either.

"I thought Ossian was coming," said Jack.

"Maybe he'll come later," said Petros, spraying crumbs from the corner of his mouth. "The low road only takes a few minutes."

However, Ossian had not put in an appearance by nearly midnight, when Uncle Doonya made it known that they would leave soon after twelve.

"But the party goes on all night," complained Petros. "Then everyone goes up to Falabray to watch the sun come up."

"We're not staying up all night." Uncle Doonya was firm. "And don't think I don't know what you've been up to, Petros. I've had a couple of friends watching you."

"What d'you mean?" Petros looked guiltily at his father.

"Let's just say I know. But I don't have to tell your mother anything, providing you behave and come home with the rest of us."

Jack turned round and saw that the far end of the hall had been cleared. Cosmo addressed the throng.

"I have one announcement: the match against Claville will be played three weeks tonight. The usual rules, but a new pitch." He nodded across the room to where Henri from Claville stood with some of his compatriots. "For those who are leaving before dawn, we wish you a Good Beltane. And may the light skies travel with you."

"Enjoy the party?" Uncle Doonya smiled.

Jack nodded. One part of him wanted to stay up and go to Falabray for the dawn, but another part was just exhausted. He got up, tugging on Petros' sleeve and indicating for him to follow. Rather more slowly, Petros also stood up and made to join the others.

As Uncle Doonya went to say goodbye to Cosmo, Jack's attention was caught by two people talking urgently by the far wall. He recognised Boreus the Kildashie, but could not for the moment place the other face.

"Who's that talking to Boreus?" he asked Petros, indicating the pair.

Petros looked across and shrugged. "Face is familiar, but dunno his name."

It was as if Boreus and the other Shian knew they were being watched. They turned, snarling as they saw Jack and the others. An icy chill ran through Jack.

"It's Rob! He was hexed by Cosmo for cheating at the wrestling."

The last time Jack had seen Rob, his face had shown abject terror as he waited for Cosmo to dish out his punishment. This time it wasn't terror on Rob's face: it was pure hatred.

14

The Claville Crew Arrive

The next morning, Jack wondered what to tell his uncle about Rob and Boreus. What had he actually seen them doing? They'd snarled at him, and he'd got that uncomfortable cold feeling, but what did that mean? Still, he couldn't get rid of a nagging feeling that something was brewing.

Jack turned his attention to obtaining the Sintura belt. His hand was healed now, so he had no excuse for sloppy tailoring, but Gilmore was not going to be easy to win round. For one thing, Fenrig was still making himself popular with the tailor, so any gifts that might have been disbursed were more likely to go to him.

Although Jack's punishment of extra lessons had finished, he found himself drifting back to Finbogie's house several evenings a week. Finbogie was much better teaching one-to-one than addressing a class of apprentices, and Jack liked practising the defences and charms that he knew his colleagues couldn't do. Jack's little store of charms and wristlets was getting too big for the small box under his bed, but the problem of persuading Gilmore to make him a Sintura belt remained.

In desperation, he turned to Freya one day as they sat down to eat their lunch. Fenrig had disappeared back to his own home, and Doxer as ever was sitting silently by himself.

"Have you ever heard of a Sintura belt?" he asked in what he hoped was a nonchalant tone.

Freya looked at him quizzically, a gleam in her eyes.

"I wonder why you'd want an expensive thing like that," she said coolly.

"So you *have* heard of it?" persisted Jack.

Freya smiled and gave a slow wink. "The thread's very rare, though," she explained. "I'm sure Gilmore's got some somewhere. But there's special charms that need to be said as you make it."

"Could you make me one?" Jack felt that the direct approach was warranted now, and he was disappointed to see Freya's eyes drop.

"But I might be able to get hold of one for you," she said after a pause. "If you make it worth my while." She looked him in the eye again.

"Can't we just call it my birthday present?" asked Jack innocently, and Freya's laugh rang out around the workshop.

"I'll see what I can do," was all she would say by way of reply.

Jack's birthday came and went with no sign of the Sintura belt. All the talk among the apprentices was of the forthcoming football match against Claville. Purdy continued to hint that she could get several of them into the Finisterre café–bar, where they would be able to see the game on what amounted to closed-circuit screens.

"There's special sceptres all the way up the High Street," Purdy explained late one afternoon as they lounged around the Shian square. "They all link together, and the pictures come up in the Finisterre."

"The humans do that too," pointed out Petros, not for the first time. "They have football games from all over the world shown in there."

"Well, we're not watching their football games," snorted Rana derisively. "This is proper football, played the Shian way. One goal settles it."

"You an expert, then?" teased Jack.

"Purdy's been telling me all about it," replied Rana confidently. "She's been seeing one of the Cos-Howe players, and he's been teaching her about tactics."

"Will Ossian be playing again this year?" asked Lizzie.

"Swackit said he'd broken his leg: that's why he wasn't at the party. But he should be playing."

"I can't see how it's the same as when they played in Claville," announced Petros. "The High Street's one big slope, and the gate at the bottom is huge. And it's made of iron, so no one will go near it to defend it. Whoever plays downhill's bound to win."

"That's why they even things up. The away team gets to choose which end to defend, so the home team get to remove one of the away team before the match begins," stated Lizzie.

"It's still a lot easier playing downhill," pointed out Jack. "Even a man down."

"There's something else about hexes," admitted Rana. "But Purdy wasn't sure what that was."

"The match is earlier this year than last year," chipped in Boyce, who had wandered along and joined them. "You said it was after the midsummer festival last year. If it's only a week away that's about a month earlier."

"It doesn't have a fixed date," explained Petros. "It's whenever they can arrange things."

"If they want to make home advantage really count," pointed out Jack, "they'd have the game in January when it's teeming down and blowing a gale. Can't see the Claville lot liking that."

However, the Claville crew picked perfect weather for their trip. They flew in a week later, landing on the field at Falabray, and made their way down the slope just before dawn. The horses were taken on to Keldy, where they could be looked after without drawing attention.

The Claville team (the "Premier crew", as Henri called it) were accompanied by a dozen or so friends and mascots. Jack and Petros were entrusted with showing Philippe, Henri's brother, around town. They accepted this duty happily, proudly showing off the city's sights.

"Which way will Claville play?" asked Jack as they strolled past St Giles' Cathedral.

"Defending the castle, of course," replied Philippe confidently. "I think it will be easy to take the ball downhill."

There had to be some reason the Cos-Howe crew had

elected to use this as the pitch, but with the away team choosing which goal to defend it seemed an uneven contest before it had even started.

That evening saw the Claville crew based in the square under the castle, where they practised moves and entertained the locals prior to the game. The home team repaired to Cos-Howe to plan strategies. Jack and the other youngsters were not invited this time, causing indignation all round.

"They let us in last year," wailed Lizzie as they sat in the square and watched the French team training. "It's not fair."

Jack was disappointed at not being allowed back into Cos-Howe, but he was more vexed that they had not yet found out how they were going to watch the match.

"You said Freya was going to get us into the Finisterre," he said accusingly to Rana.

"She's gone to Cos-Howe with Purdy." Rana sounded despondent. "I thought she'd have said by now. Purdy's friend said the entrance had to be kept a secret."

"But we won't take up much room," said Jack. "We can always squeeze up if there's not much space."

"I like squeezing up," noted Lizzie, sounding happier. "It feels funny, but it's nice, you know?"

Rana had wandered off a little and was eyeing up one of the French players. Sensing he was being watched, he turned and smiled, causing Rana to blush. Philippe had observed this little encounter and approached.

"You were speaking with him last year, no?"

Rana's flushed face showed no sign of lessening. "He was just telling us about Claville. We'd never been to France before."

"I have been in Edinburgh three times now," announced Philippe. "It is a good city, but very noisy."

"What were the other matches like?"

"Very tough. Always there would be broken heads or legs. But we bring a good physician, and all Claville Shian know how to heal wounds."

"Maybe Ossian should have come to Edinburgh to get his leg fixed by the Claville physician," said Lizzie thoughtfully.

"What time will it start?" asked Rana.

"Ten o'clock. Then we will — how do you say? — slow things up."

"Slow things *down*," corrected Rana. She paused. "How are you going to see the game?"

"Henri says I will go to the top of one of the buildings. There is a café in the building used by some Shian."

"The Finisterre?" gasped Rana. "Can you get us in there too?"

"I will see. I must ask my brother."

Grandpa Sandy ambled out of the house and joined the youngsters by the side of the square.

"I trust our visitors do not think you are spying on their training," he said with a chuckle, looking across to where Henri was talking with his players.

Catching Grandpa Sandy's gaze, Henri nodded. Without ceremony, the French contingent gathered together into a huddle, and Grandpa Sandy joined then.

Jack watched despondently.

"Can't we just go up to the High Street and watch?" he said to no one in particular.

His thoughts were interrupted by the arrival of a small winged creature, which flew up to Rana and Lizzie.

"It's a grig!" said Lizzie excitedly. The tiny creature perched on Rana's ear and whispered to her.

"Freya says we're to meet her at the Finisterre," announced Rana happily. "She'll get us in."

Jack looked across at Petros, who didn't like making outward shows of his feelings, but he too was beaming from ear to ear.

Within seconds they had passed through the Shian gate, emerging onto the castle esplanade at human height. The late evening sky was still bright, but it was cold. Lizzie shivered involuntarily.

"We won't need coats where we're going," proclaimed Rana happily as she set off at pace towards the High Street.

They reached the Finisterre within a few minutes and were relieved to see Freya standing outside where tourists and locals milled around. Jack and the others edged nervously through the human crowd to where Freya was standing, a nonchalant look on her face.

"We thought you'd forgotten about us," said Lizzie. "The players will be ready to start soon."

"I said I'd get you in, didn't I?" Freya was playing it cool.

"How, then?" asked Jack. He remembered how Philippe had taken them into the town hall in Claville, but that had been up a dimly lit side street, with no one nearby. This was the Edinburgh High Street, with dozens of humans all around.

"Nobody sees what they don't expect to see," said Freya. "They're looking out for young people trying to get in the pub, so you can't just walk in. But we use the Shian door. Just copy me."

Freya walked up to the side wall of the Finisterre, just next to one of the windows that looked onto the High Street. A small crowd of human women stood there shivering; all wore identical T-shirts, with "End of the Road" on the back and "Tina's Last Fling" on the front. One of them had a large red L stuck to her back. Glancing both ways to ensure that the others could see what she was doing, Freya placed her right hand on a part of the stone wall that was more worn than the surrounding area, and leant forward.

"*Effatha!*"

In a fraction of a second, Freya had fallen through the wall.

Tina, with the L on her back, blinked and looked uncertainly at the remaining youngsters.

"That's it?" exclaimed Jack incredulously. "The same charm we use to get into the square?"

"You have to know where the key stone is," pointed out Petros, but he was just as surprised as Jack.

They each quickly followed Freya's example, one by one falling through the wall. Tina blinked twice, and swayed.

"I've had enough," she hiccupped to her friends. "Put me to bed."

15
Shian Football

Jack smelt stale beer.

"Not that way." Petros dragged him by the arm away from a narrow corridor that led to the pub. "That's the humans' bit. We're down here."

Shrinking back to Shian height, they passed through a small door on the right, one that was almost invisible in the gloomy light. Entering, Jack was struck by how large the room was. There must have been forty or fifty Shian gathered there on benches, all facing Jack as he entered. Looking nervously behind him, he saw a series of hazy moving pictures that flickered on a row of canvas screens.

"Get out of the way!" shouted a voice from the back.

Petros steered Jack away to where Rana, Lizzie and Freya were seated around a small table; Purdy stood, slightly apart, watching the screen intently. Behind the counter stood a Darrig pouring clear fluid into a row of tiny glasses.

"How long before it starts?" asked Jack. He felt his heart quicken as the thought of the match crept over him.

"A few minutes," said Freya calmly. Then she leant over towards Jack and gave him a small kiss on the cheek. "Happy birthday," she said quietly, and slipped something silk-like into his hand.

Jack looked down. At first he couldn't figure out what it was. Then it dawned on him.

"A Sintura belt!" he exclaimed happily. "You made one."

"Acquired one," replied Freya with a broad grin. "But don't go telling. It's a secret, right? There's a hair wristlet in there too. It'll see you right."

Jack hastily stuffed the belt into his pocket. It was so light to the touch that he could hardly feel it.

The attention of the others around the table was moved to the doorway, through which a tall figure had just emerged. Again the exasperated shout came from the back: "Get – out – of – the – way!"

There was a cheer as this echoed around the room, then the crowd fell silent as they saw that it was Matthew who had entered. He stepped forward, a tattered leather book in his hand, and addressed the assembled Shian.

"Welcome to the match between Cos-Howe and Claville. This is the five hundred and thirty-ninth encounter, and I am pleased to say that I have refereed over two hundred of these. For the first time in Edinburgh, the pitch is to be your Royal Mile.

"The rules are the same as ever. As spectators, you must not assist or hinder in any way. Claville have elected to defend the castle gate; Cos-Howe have used their right to remove one

Claville player, so Henri will not play. He has gone to watch the game with his brother. The away team's hexes will last one minute, the home team's two minutes. I will shortly freeze time for the match."

As Matthew left, the screens became more focussed. Each showed a different section of the High Street and the streets running parallel to it. Matthew's image came into the centre screen.

One of the Cos-Howe supporters got up and began to move towards the door under the screens.

"Oi! You're in the way!"

The figure stopped and turned around. He glared at the back of the room, from where the shout had come.

"It's Rob." Jack nudged Petros, who had been looking intently at the screens. "Don't you remember? He was talking with Boreus at Cos-Howe."

Jack thought back to the wrestling match at Cos-Howe the previous year, when Rob had used a charm stone to blind his opponent. Cosmo had intervened, using a paralysing hex. The memory of Rob's terrified eyes returned to Jack. But now there was no terror: Jack could sense his hatred.

As Rob disappeared through the door, the figure of Matthew approached the busy road junction where St Margaret's Street crosses the High Street and held his sceptre aloft. A glow emanated from it, and Jack could see that all the cars and human figures on the screens had frozen. Then Matthew sketched a pattern in the air, and the fiery outline of a chalice appeared, hanging some six feet from the ground.

"What's the charm he uses to do that?" enquired Freya.

"'Calixignis'," replied Jack smugly. "Cosmo told me after the game last year."

A figure stuck his head around the door.

"Is Jack here? Jack Shian?"

Exchanging a puzzled look with Petros, Jack put up his hand.

"You're wanted. Quickly!"

Jack clambered down towards the door and disappeared.

"He's going to miss the game!" exclaimed Lizzie. "It's just starting!"

A cluster of four Claville players approached Matthew, as did three Cos-Howe players, led by Cosmo, their long cloaks flapping in the breeze. Matthew addressed both groups, after which there was a short pause, and then he threw the ball up.

Cosmo jumped as his teammates Oobit and Tom drew their sceptres and made to hex the Claville players. *A repeat of last year's start*, thought Petros, but he hadn't reckoned on the French response. Before the Cos-Howe hexes could be fired, the four Claville players clapped their hands above their heads and disappeared. Cosmo seemed unsure of what to do: he stood, holding the ball, and seemed to be arguing with his teammates.

"They must've used too much hex," said Petros. "They've obliterated them."

"I don't think so," said Lizzie, looking intently at the screen next to the centre one. "They're just drawing the Cos-Howe team on. Look – Claville's formed up around the next crossroads."

"It's a trap!" exclaimed Rana. "They'll let the Cos-Howe boys get tired out running uphill, then counter-attack."

Indeed, after the unexpected start, the Cos-Howe contingent were moving quickly up to the next intersection, passing immobilised humans, but apparently unaware of why they were meeting so little French resistance.

"Look – there's the Claville crew. They're hiding in those doorways. Cosmo's been suckered."

There was a murmur of agreement around the room.

Then the hexes started to fly.

The middle left screen became bright orange as the Claville trap was sprung. The beleaguered Cos-Howe players dived for the cover of doorways and immobile cars, as the hexes flew in from left and right.

"They haven't a hope," said Rana. "This is going to be over before it's even begun."

"It was better seeing it live last year," complained Lizzie. "You can't see so much on the screens."

"There was loads we missed last year because we couldn't see it from the roof," pointed out Petros. "The screens are great: you can see almost all of it."

But what they could see was not very cheering: the Cos-Howe team were pinned down, facing an enemy with the advantage of height. While the doorways and cars offered some protection, it seemed only a matter of time before they were hexed one by one.

Lizzie's eyes had narrowed. "Who's got the ball?"

"Cosmo had it," said Rana. "There he is. He'll have it under his cloak."

Cosmo's distinctive frame had been clearly visible near the centre of the besieged Cos-Howe group as they moved uphill. They had nearly made it as far as the North Bridge crossroad, but had been forced to retreat under the onslaught of hexes from the Claville ambush.

"This is hopeless," said Petros despondently. "They're pinned down. Claville will pick them off and then just wander down to the palace."

"What does that screen there cover?" asked Rana, pointing at the next screen to the one showing the ambush in progress. She was staring intently at two figures moving furtively down a nearly deserted street.

"That's the Cowmarket," said Freya, moving closer. "Below the High Street."

"Ooh, it's Jack," shouted Purdy, becoming suddenly animated as a face came into focus on the screen. "He's got a sceptre. And Gandie's with him."

"How come Jack's playing?" demanded Petros. "And why are they there? They should be up on the High Street helping their team."

"They are," said Rana excitedly. "It's all a trick: Cosmo's drawn the Claville fire while they get the ball along to the Grassmarket. Then they can go up Castle Wynd steps to the esplanade. I'll bet Claville haven't got more than one player defending the castle goal: they don't think anyone'll get that far."

Rana was right. A quick glance at the left-hand screen showed a solitary Claville player sitting on the castle esplanade. He looked very bored.

As foreseen, Gandie and Jack reached the Grassmarket and began climbing. The two players were lost to sight for a few moments as they ascended the steps, then they were seen to emerge, puffing slightly, at the top. Glancing to their right, they saw the bulk of the Claville crew some distance away, facing down the High Street, battling with the beleaguered Cos-Howe team. They smiled at each other as they turned left to go up to the esplanade.

Their backs close to the nearside wall, they edged cautiously up towards the castle. Catching sight of the solitary Claville player as he sat, bored, in the centre of the esplanade, Jack motioned to Gandie to remain hidden. Jack then stuck his sceptre down the back of his cloak and walked out boldly onto the esplanade, his hands out to the sides. The Claville player saw him approach and got uncertainly to his feet.

"I did not see you training before the match."

"A late substitute. One of our players got ill," said Jack casually as he drew near to his opponent. "Your team have us pinned down back there." His hands remained visible and weapon-free.

The Claville player smiled. "Better tactics for us, I think?"

"Perhaps," said Jack. "But only if they work." In a flash he had scooped out his sceptre and pointed it at the surprised Claville player.

"*Attonitus!*" A spark flew from the sceptre, and the Claville man fell back without a sound.

Seeing this, Gandie trotted out from where he had been sheltering and kicked the ball up to Jack. Between them they played keepy-uppy a few times as they moved without opposition towards the castle gate. Seeing that statue-like tourists partially blocked the view of the gate, Jack placed the ball on the ground and indicated to Gandie to act as goalkeeper. As he lined up to take the free kick, Matthew appeared as if out of nowhere.

Jack retreated a few paces, then ran up and struck the ball. It curved up, just clearing the humans' heads, then down again towards the gate. In an extravagant display of incompetence, Gandie pretended to try to save the shot. He fell in a crumpled heap, turning his head to watch the ball strike the castle gate.

Petros and the others, watching in the Finisterre, let out a roar of joy as the goal was scored. Matthew, standing just yards from the goal, held up his sceptre and shot a bolt into the sky, signalling that the game was over. Within seconds, the hex-fight at North Bridge ceased. Jack scooped up the ball and handed it to Matthew, and together the three of them walked back across the esplanade. Encountering the prostrate Claville player, Jack and Gandie picked him up and made their way back down to the North Bridge crossroads. Several hexed players lay motionless on the ground. The rest of the puzzled Claville players stood around the High Street, unsure about what had happened.

Cosmo emerged from the shelter of a doorway, grinning. Gandie walked up to him and they embraced, clapping each other on the back.

"It worked then," said Cosmo happily. "Well done, Jack. Your speed along the Grassmarket was what we needed."

Jack beamed with pride as Henri approached, a look of disappointment on his face.

"Ah, you tricked us," he said sadly.

"You started it," replied Cosmo happily. "All that show about retreating at the beginning."

Henri had to concede that the Claville bluff had been bettered by the home team's stratagem.

"I felt sure that we could win, playing down the hill."

"Things aren't always what they seem," replied Gandie with a grin.

"I couldn't let you know before the game," said Cosmo to Jack. "The Claville boys were watching our training. You were our secret weapon."

Those players who had been hexed were starting to come round, and there was a general hubbub as the game was discussed.

"My friends," declared Matthew, "we have witnessed a fascinating game tonight, a game of ploys and deceits. I congratulate the home team. I am sure that the party back at Cos-Howe will be memorable. Sadly, I cannot join you for that. The time is set to return to normal for the humans in fifteen minutes; by then you should all be safely back at Cos-Howe."

The players began to walk down the High Street, and were soon mingling with the crowd that was pouring out from the Finisterre. Excited chatter and complaints about the strategies used by both sides were mixed. Purdy ran out and gave Jack a big hug.

Cosmo approached the fiery outline that still hung in the air.

"We thank our friends for coming from Claville," he said happily. "You are all invited to join us at Cos-Howe." He reached up to grasp the chalice, which, as it had done the year before, vanished as soon as it was touched.

Jack joined the rousing cheer that went up from the home players. In the commotion, he didn't see Matthew simply disappearing along with the Chalice.

The crowd turned down St Margaret's Street and made for

Cos-Howe. Walking arm in arm with Jack, Purdy's face showed her delight in the game's outcome and his part in it. Within ten minutes they were near the safety of Cos-Howe, but the last few yards were a mad dash as the skies darkened and heavy rain began to fall. Thunderclaps echoed from building to building as the stragglers made their way in.

Despite the sudden wintry blast, the High Street resumed its usual activities, with none of the humans any the wiser about the events that had so recently taken place there. There were broken glasses and several cracked windows in the pavement bars around the North Bridge crossroads, and several smears of blood on the ground where a hex had worked too well. But as the humans retreated indoors to escape the rain, none thought to challenge these things: it was a Saturday evening, after all.

At Cos-Howe, the party was getting into full swing. Players swapped stories of hexes delivered and rebuffed, of injuries sustained and of opponents vanquished. Jack, supplied with a large goblet of juniper juice, was regaling his cousins – again – with stories of how fast he'd had to run along the Grassmarket and how puffed he'd been by the time he climbed all the steps to the castle.

"Ambush!"

There was a cheer from the assembled Cos-Howe players and supporters as a ragged figure ran in amongst them shouting.

"We know," shouted Gandie, waving his arm extravagantly. "But the smart ones got out of the way. And we won."

"*Ambush!*"

The cry was more insistent. Then Jack saw that it was

Armina who was shouting. Her tall frame was almost doubled over as she staggered around in a blind panic.

"The Kildashie," she spluttered, "have taken the Congress."

Silence.

Then screams.

16
Escape to Dunvik

Cos–Howe was in a state of uproar, and it was several minutes before Cosmo's pleas for quiet had the desired effect.

"Tell us what happened," he said firmly to Armina, who had collapsed onto a chair.

Armina looked up at him.

"They will come here," she gasped. "They know that you will resist them; they will try to kill you."

"What are we to the Congress?" demanded a voice. "They tried to ban us having the match in the High Street. A fight between the Kildashie and the Congress is not our affair."

Cosmo turned and fixed the speaker with a beady eye.

"The Kildashie are Unseelie. If they take the Shian square, they can get the Stone and the Chalice. Then nothing will stop them."

"The Kildashie know there is a low road entrance here." Armina's voice was weak.

"How did they take the Congress?" demanded Oobit.

"Our meeting was at Falabray. Suddenly, the air froze, and they were all around us. One of your men was with them."

"Who?"

"His name is Rob, I think. But there was no sound."

"No sound!" shouted Tom. "Then they have the Tassitus charm. It's as good as being invisible."

"Calm down, Tom," said Cosmo bluntly. Then he turned to Armina. "Is anyone killed?"

"Atholmor – I think. And Tomte the dwarf. He tried to fight, but there were too many. The rest are killed or captured."

"And how d'you get away, then?" sneered Tom. "If you were surrounded?"

Armina's gasps lightened. She stood up slowly and fixed Tom with a piercing glare. Tom looked away uncomfortably.

Then Jack saw the blood.

"Armina!" He ran forward and guided the enchantress back into the chair. "Please help!" he shouted behind him.

A Claville supporter stepped forward and produced a linen cloth, which he deftly wrapped around Armina's upper arm, staunching the blood. Then, taking a small vial from his cloak, he dribbled some oil over Armina's whole arm. There was a puff of blue smoke.

"You believe Tig will come here with his warriors?" demanded Cosmo.

"Not Tig," replied Armina, wincing in pain. "Boreus. He boasted that Tig and Donar were dead. Boreus brought in many more Kildashie; he controls them now."

Jack's scalp felt icy cold. *That Boreus . . . he was always a menace . . . Without Tig around to keep him in order . . .* Jack gritted his teeth.

"You must stop them," begged Armina. "They may not risk a full assault on the square, but if they can get in from here, then all is lost."

"We'll stop them," said Cosmo calmly. "But you need to get away. And someone needs to protect the Stone Room, in case they get into the castle."

Armina's gaze fell upon Jack and Rana.

"You – you must take me to your grandfather. We must warn him."

Rana looked uncertainly at her cousin.

"Come on," said Jack simply. He helped Armina back up.

"Your arm will heal," said the Claville physician to Armina as she tottered forward. "You know what to do. Here I must stay: if there will be fighting, I am needed."

Lizzie had gone pale; her right arm started to shake. Rana moved over to her, and took her arm gently. She pulled her sister along after Jack, who was steering Armina toward to the low road entrance.

"I'll come too," said Petros. "Freya, you'd better take Purdy to your mum and dad."

Within seconds they had all reached the low road and were whisked along to the Shian square.

The news had got there first.

Good old grigs, thought Jack.

Uncle Doonya was in earnest conversation with his neighbour Festus and a Darrig Jack didn't think he'd ever seen before. Aunt Katie stood at the front door, looking anxiously towards the low road entrance. When she saw the youngsters, she let out a scream of joy.

Rana and Lizzie made their way quickly to their mother, while Petros looked rather sheepishly at Jack. However, Jack's full concentration was on getting Armina up to her house. She walked painfully, making Jack wonder what other injuries she had sustained.

Uncle Doonya strode over to Petros.

"We'll have to get Grandpa out of here. Pack what you can carry for him. We'll leave in two minutes."

Petros, relieved to have someone take control, ran towards the house, but was met at the door by his grandfather. When Armina saw him, she stopped.

"We must protect the Stone Room."

Grandpa Sandy nodded.

"Petros, you can take us to the Stone Room," he said simply. "We can place a series of hexes that will stop the Kildashie – for now. Then we must leave. We'll go to Keldy."

Jack watched as Petros led Grandpa Sandy and Armina, both shuffling awkwardly, towards the side wall of the square. Once there, Grandpa Sandy placed his sceptre on the ground, and they all seemed to melt into the rock.

If I've got to leave, thought Jack, *I'm taking my things with me*.

He ran upstairs, grabbed his work satchel and stuffed a few clothes inside. Then he took the Sintura belt from his pocket and examined it briefly. With all the excitement of the match, and the party, he hadn't given his birthday present another thought. Feather-light, it was almost a yard long and had a series of small pouches along the side. Quickly, he rummaged in the box under his bed and filled the pouches with the charms and hexes Finbogie had given him.

Finbogie: he was in the Congress. Has he been killed? Armina wasn't sure.

"Jack! Get a move on! We have to leave now." Aunt Katie's voice was insistent.

Jack wound the Sintura belt around his waist and secured it. Despite being crammed, it weighed next to nothing. Then Jack remembered:

My vococorn!

Locating the prized ram's horn Tamlina had given him, Jack realised instantly that it was much too big to take. Even the Sintura belt wouldn't cope with that. Prising up a loose floorboard, Jack thrust the horn underneath it. Grabbing his satchel, he ran downstairs.

The square was packed. Shian were filing down towards the low road entrance; others milled around anxiously. Jack caught sight of his uncle.

"We must get you lot out of here. The Kildashie could be here any minute."

"Will they get into the square then, Dad?" Petros had returned from his brief errand to the Stone Room.

"We're not taking any chances: they obviously believe that with the Congress defeated they'll have free rein. Grandpa and Armina aren't fit to fight. We must get them away."

"Are we going to Keldy?"

"We'll be safe there. Once we've regrouped, we can work out how to get back. And don't worry about the manuscripts – I've hidden them."

Jack took his grandfather's arm and gave it a squeeze.

"I'll carry this, Grandpa," he said simply, loosing his grandfather's grip on the bag he was clutching.

"I'll take Armina along to the low road. She's grabbed a few things from her house. I'll tell you about the Stone Room later," Petros added with a grin.

The crowd had broken into small groups and was steadily disappearing along the low road. Petros led Armina along, helped by Lizzie and Aunt Katie.

"See you in Keldy," declared Petros, as the four of them stepped onto the mound.

"We'll come last," announced Uncle Doonya, indicating the Darrig. "Make sure everyone else is away safely."

Jack and Rana shepherded their grandfather up onto the mound of earth that marked the low road.

"I'll do it," announced Jack confidently. He stepped onto the mound and ushered Rana and Grandpa Sandy up beside him. Gripping both their waists, he called out, "Wind-flock Dunvik!"

It was like the time they'd gone up to Keldy two months earlier. The howling and moaning were loud and insistent. After the mild air of May, the wind that whipped around them was freezing and the spinning sensation was violent. The journey took nearly twenty minutes, and for the first time in many trips, Jack felt sick. He felt Rana grip his arm tightly.

At last the spinning slowed down, and they came to rest within the ruined hermit's cell at Dunvik. Grandpa Sandy immediately collapsed onto the ground, gasping.

"Grandpa!" called Rana, her voice quavering.

"I'll be all right. Need to rest for a while."

Rana turned on Jack.

"We were supposed to go to Keldy," she snapped. "Why d'you bring us here?"

"I . . . I don't know. Something must've made me think this was better." Jack felt confused. It was dark, an almost moonless night, and a steady drizzle fell.

"There's nothing here," shouted Rana angrily. "Just an old ruin. Mum'll be worried sick when we don't arrive in Keldy."

Jack knelt down to attend to his grandfather, whose breathing had become laboured.

"Grandpa, can I get you anything?"

Grandpa Sandy's breathing slowly eased, and he propped himself up against the rocks of the ancient cell wall.

"I can't manage another low road trip tonight. We'll have to stay here." His voice croaked slightly.

"I've got your bag," said Jack, unsure what else to say.

"Jack," said Grandpa between gasps, "tell me: what made you bring us here?"

"The name just came out," replied Jack unhappily. "I didn't mean to. It just happened."

Grandpa Sandy thought for a few moments. "Maybe later we'll find out why. In the meantime, we can shelter in the old castle. Jack, can you get me that big stick there?" He pointed to part of a dead branch that lay on the ground.

Jack fetched the stick and helped his grandfather to his feet. Though unsteady, Grandpa Sandy started to shuffle through the forest towards the old castle, the scene of the great fight with the Brashat in the early hours of Hallows' Day.

Jack and Rana followed on. The previous year they had run this distance, all the way from the prince's cave to the clearing before the castle. Now it felt like they were going at a snail's pace. The rain was getting heavier, and by the time they reached the clearing, they were all thoroughly wet.

"The scene of your great triumph," said Grandpa Sandy quietly as they crossed the clearing. There was no evidence of the battle. The amphitheatre that had materialised to accommodate the Shian commonwealth had disappeared, and the clearing was flat once more.

The old castle was unchanged: although dilapidated, and positively dangerous in places, a few rooms were reasonably wind- and watertight.

Jack dragged a few dead branches from the forest floor and prepared them in the ancient hall's fireplace. The fire's glow brought flickering shadows to the room, but they were all grateful for the heat, and despite the smoke he and Grandpa Sandy crouched as near as they could to the flames. Rana returned from a short inspection of the castle and announced that she could find no food or bedding.

"It's late," announced Grandpa, looking and sounding exhausted. "I'll put a bell hex around the castle so we're not disturbed. We can use the low road when it gets light. I suggest we all try to get some rest."

Using their bags as pillows, they curled up on the floor in the flickering light. It was strange being inside. Jack had only seen the castle from the outside before. *What secrets does it hold?* he wondered. From its evil human owner and the terror he'd brought to the local people to the Brashat camping in it while they hunted the King's Chalice. If the walls could speak, what stories would they tell?

Jack's thoughts got no further. A deep and dreamless sleep

arrived, and it felt like only a few minutes before he was waking to bright sunshine that streamed in through the large ruined windows.

"Did you sleep well?" Grandpa Sandy was shaking him by the arm.

Jack rubbed his eyes and yawned. He sat up and peered around him.

"We're at Dunvik Castle," announced Grandpa Sandy helpfully, seeing his look of bewilderment. "You've had a good sleep. I wish I could say the same."

"I'm hungry," stated Jack. "Can we get some breakfast?"

"Let's wake Rana, and we'll go back to the low road. We can eat at Keldy."

It took several minutes to rouse Rana. Having made sure that the fire had burnt itself out, Grandpa Sandy dissolved the bell hex that had protected the castle overnight, and they set off back to the hermit's cell. Grandpa Sandy still limped, but managed to make reasonable progress with his walking stick.

They had only gone a few yards into the forest when Jack felt the muscles beside his eyes start to twitch.

"Something's not right," he announced, stopping dead in his tracks.

"What now?" complained Rana. "Let's just get to Keldy."

A cackling sound came from their right. Jack turned to look. Although the sun was up, it was still gloomy in the forest, and it took his eyes a few seconds to locate the source of the noise. A shiver ran up his spine. A Dunter.

The old man glared maliciously at the three of them, then took off his cap and threw it. Drops of blood sprayed out, one falling on Grandpa's arm, sizzling as it landed.

"*Absango!*" Jack thrust out his right arm and flicked his wrist. There was a loud pop and the Dunter vanished, leaving behind only a sickly smell of blood.

"Where d'you learn that?" asked Rana, clearly impressed.

"We can discuss it later," stated Grandpa. "If there's more of his kind around, we need to get away." A pungent smell arose from his arm.

They hurried as quickly as Grandpa Sandy's condition allowed, and within a few minutes were at the hermit's cell. Their relief at reaching their destination was short-lived, however: its low walls had been dislodged and scattered, the ground in the centre of the cell had been dug up, and there were signs of a fire.

Jack stared with disbelief, then looked at his grandfather. His worst fears were quickly confirmed.

"We can't use the low road," stated Grandpa Sandy. "It's been sabotaged."

17
Konan Arbormal

"What are we going to do?" asked Rana miserably. "I want to see Mum."

"The low road's out of action," answered Grandpa Sandy flatly. He sagged a little, leaning more heavily on his crude walking stick.

"Can't we get some breakfast?" said Jack. "I'm hungry."

"I'm sure food would do us all good. What do you propose?"

"Fish. Last time we were here, Ossian said the dark loch has huge fish."

"Dunters won't go near salt water. Fish sounds like a good idea."

"I'm good at fishing," proclaimed Rana, brightening up. "Just get me a stick and some twine. You two can get a fire going."

"The loch's down this way," announced Jack, setting off

quickly towards the prince's cave. He had just got past it when he came to a sudden halt. Rana caught up with him, panting, "Not so fast. Grandpa can't keep up."

Then she caught the look in Jack's eyes.

"What's wrong? You look like you've seen a ghost."

Jack was staring at an oak tree not ten yards away. His face had gone pale, and he felt sweat break out on his forehead. His lips moved, but no more than a mumble emerged. Rana's eyes followed his gaze, and reality dawned.

"Oh! Is that Konan's tree?"

Jack's mind was filled with the memory of the struggle they'd had on this very spot just a few months earlier, when Konan had threatened to break both their necks.

"Dad fused Konan into that oak," whispered Rana.

Jack nodded. "We used the Aximon and broke free. We'd have been standing just here."

As Rana went back to fetch their grandfather, Jack's eye was caught by a twinkle on the ground. Stooping down, he found a small sand timer. Encased in a brass fitting, it had an emerald at either end. Whichever way Jack turned it, the glass remained vertical, the sands falling. He slipped the timer into his pocket.

Grandpa Sandy appeared with Rana and appraised the scene.

"So that's why you brought us here," he said quietly.

Jack's mind was still racing. Had he brought them here because he wanted to see Konan again? No, not see him. Damage him, possibly. Or interrogate him.

"Can we get him to tell us . . ."

"I don't think so, Jack." His grandfather placed his hand on

Jack's shoulder. "He may well be able to hear. But we'd need to know what kind of counter-hex would make him speak."

"Armina knows stuff about counter-hexes," said Rana simply.

"Unfortunately," replied her grandfather, wincing, "Armina is not here. I could do with her help myself. The low road journey was hard going, and my arm feels sore now." A foul reek rose from his arm, which steamed gently. He grimaced as another spasm ran through him.

"I read some of the papers on her desk while we were visiting you, though. There wasn't much to do when you were asleep."

Grandpa Sandy turned to her.

"Do you mean to say you know how to make an Arbormal speak?"

"Arbormal?"

"A treeman – a Shian fused with a tree."

"Well," began Rana, suddenly less sure of herself, "I remember there was a charm called a Sylvox, but there's something else too, something about the tree's resistance. Once you fix that, you make the treeman speak."

Grandpa Sandy thought for a few moments. "There's different charms for different trees," he mused. "For an oak, I guess it would be 'Quercus'."

"Let's try it then," urged Jack. "If he can speak, maybe he can tell us where my dad is."

"We may only get one question, Jack, so we'll need to plan this carefully. Let's eat first and think about it."

Secretly Jack would have liked to take an axe to the Konan

oak to have something to burn, but he sensed this might be counterproductive. Aware that his grandfather was still weak, Jack did not pester him to help as he collected firewood.

Rana had quickly found a thin branch for a rod, and Grandpa had unravelled some thread from the bottom of his cloak, following which he had simply stretched himself out on the ground. Fashioning a crude hook out of a pin she had in her pocket, Rana went down to the loch side to dig for worms.

Her expertise soon paid off, and within half an hour two brown trout lay sizzling on the fire Jack had started. The smell was tantalising, and Jack took pleasure in watching the smoke curling around the two fish. The skin bubbled with the heat, and juices ran down into the fire, spitting and sizzling. Idly, Jack stuffed some dirt from the ground into the jomo bag on his Sintura belt.

Once they had all eaten, they returned to the plan for enabling the Quercus charm.

"My mind's not thinking straight," said Grandpa, rubbing his arm. "But I believe we're here to find something out. So we need to get it right. What do we need to know?"

"Where my dad is," said Jack simply.

"Or where the Sphere is," pointed out Rana.

"When the Grey captured Konan, he was looking for the Chalice, not the Sphere," pointed out Grandpa. "Jack's right. We'll ask him where Phineas is."

"Or how he got away from being suspended," added Rana.

"We'll come to that if we've time," answered her grandfather.

Jack stared at the oak. For a while he could see no trace of

Konan. Slowly, his eyes became focussed on a particular part of the trunk, and he convinced himself that two knots in the wood were closed eyes and a gash in the bark below was a grimacing mouth. Further down the trunk were several long vertical slashes, an inch or so apart.

"So how d'you wake him up?" Jack asked.

Grandpa collected his thoughts for a moment, then pointed his sceptre at the oak.

"*Quercus!*"

A feeble ray emerged from the sceptre, and the tree glowed briefly.

"It's not working. Or I'm not strong enough to make it work."

Jack looked around in frustration. Spying a large dead branch nearby, he picked it up and ran at the tree. Reaching it, he hit the trunk hard.

The tree began to fizzle.

"I've remembered!" shouted Rana. "You wake the tree up first, then use the Quercus charm. And you shout 'Mortogoon'."

"Of course!" Grandpa Sandy held his forehead. "Just as well someone here is alert. First 'Mortogoon', *then* the Quercus charm."

"Can't I be the one to hit him?" Rana spoke up. "He tried to kill me too."

"It's my dad we're trying to find," stated Jack, gripping the branch tightly and thinking about where would be best to strike the tree trunk.

"The side of his head," said his grandfather, reading his thoughts. "I'm ready now."

Jack checked the grip on his branch and looked up at his grandfather.

"Mortogoon?"

Grandpa Sandy nodded.

Jack was filled with a certainty that in a few moments he would find out where his father was. He got set, retreated a few paces, then ran screaming at the tree. As he hit the side of the trunk, he yelled, "*Mortogoon!*"

Immediately his grandfather stepped forward with his sceptre and called out, "*Quercus!*"

As the bolt shot forward, Jack moved back, wondering what would happen next. To his surprise, he could see the two knots of wood moving . . . Yes, blinking. The gash in the wood below them shifted a little, and a rumbling came from within the tree.

"Konan, I am Sandy of the Stone. I command you to tell me where Phineas of Rangie is kept by the Grey."

No further sound came from the tree.

"Konan, tell me where Phineas of Rangie is."

Grandpa Sandy's second command was no more effective than the first.

"The Kildashie have taken the Shian square." Jack spoke firmly, facing the tree directly.

The knots of wood shifted again, and the gash began to move.

"A plague on both your houses."

It was a strange sound. Dry and harsh, like someone whose mouth was a stranger to liquid.

"If you don't tell us," said Jack in exasperation, "we'll . . . we'll burn you. You'll die slowly."

"I do not fear death."

"How'd you escape, then?" shouted Rana.

"I stopped time flying . . ."

We need to find this out, it's important. It's right. Jack's mind raced. *But something's missing, something that helped us last year.* Who had been around?

Suddenly his mind cleared, and he faced the tree again with a new determination, his right eye blazing. Holding out his right palm he shouted, "*Gosol!*"

A ray shot from his hand and engulfed the tree. It glowed for a few moments, and when this faded a low creaking sound came from within. The sound built slowly, increasing in pitch and volume until it was almost too loud to bear. Rana covered her ears and closed her eyes, trying to block it out. And then it stopped.

There was complete silence.

Then Konan's voice began again, but it was different. Still hostile, but less harsh.

"Marco . . . urrgghh . . . by Loch na Keal's water . . . Stone key . . . Raglan . . ."

The tree appeared to shudder, and the voice stopped. For several minutes there was no sound at all. Then Jack saw that the knots and the gash had stopped moving.

"He will say no more." Grandpa Sandy's voice was firm.

"Let's burn him, then," said Rana. "He doesn't deserve to live."

"Cosmo stopped your father from killing him last year, Rana. We do not have that right."

Jack felt deflated and confused.

"Grandpa, this is hopeless."

"So you think Konan didn't make any sense?" said his grandfather. "To be truthful, I'm surprised at how much he *did* say."

"He told us nothing," shouted Jack. "It didn't make any sense."

"He said little," replied Grandpa Sandy with a twinkle in his eye, "but he told us a great deal."

18
Aquine Ride

"What?" Jack's voice was near to breaking, the ache in his heart was so great. "He was supposed to tell us about my father. He just said Marco, or something. What's that mean? And what's Loch na Keal's water?"

"There is a legend of a great cat, a mystical beast known as Marco, on a small island called Ilanbeg. It's down the coast near Loch na Keal – a sea loch, like this one."

Cats! Jack shuddered. Ordinary ones were bad enough. He had no inclination to tackle a great one.

"Well, what about Stone key and 'Raglan'?"

"'Stone key' is just an old Shian legend that someday Shian will find a key that gives them the power of the Stone. It's not true – but Konan must have believed it was. He spoke the truth when you used Gosol on him – he had no option."

"But Tamlina mentioned Raglan last year: when she was in a trance, and then when she zapped Petros."

"Tamlina's riddles are famous; most of the time nobody knows what she means."

"So how does this help us find my father?"

"The Stone key doesn't, but Loch na Keal does: we were meant to find this out. That's why you brought us here."

"If we'd told Konan the Kildashie have captured Fenrig and Morrigan, he might have helped us more," added Rana. "They're Brashat too."

"We don't know if they were captured, though," pointed out Jack. "They're hardly ever around. Olbeg's no idea where they are most of the time."

"I've no great liking for young Fenrig or his sister, but I hope they managed to get away from the square," replied Grandpa Sandy. "But I'm afraid that Konan is no more use to us now."

"So we have to find this island, then?" asked Rana. "Can't we go to Keldy?"

"The hermit cell low road is out of action, and we have no horses. Getting to Keldy will take many days. I cannot move fast, or far, over land. But we are by the sea; we can sail down the coast."

"How?" demanded Jack. He still couldn't understand how this would move them forward. "We don't have a boat."

"Jack, I'm surprised at you. Hasn't Murkle told you about the sea creatures?"

"He just goes on about giants and trolls. He's so boring."

"Nothing about Aquines, then?"

"Dad told me about them," piped up Rana. "They're sea horses."

"Of a kind," replied Grandpa Sandy. "Not like the kelpie in

Loch Keldy, though. Aquines are good-natured beasts. If we can call them, they may give us a lift down the coast."

Grandpa set to gathering roots and leaves. Mixing them in with some fish scales, he pounded them down into a paste before adding it to some water in a small phial he took from his cloak.

"Aren't there any other low road entrances?" Rana's voice was flat, without real hope. "Then we could join the others in Keldy."

"Digging the ground up, and the fire, that was sabotage. Any other entrances nearby will have been destroyed too. Our best bet is to get down the coast."

The three set out along the shoreline towards the open sea. As they walked, Grandpa Sandy explained how the coastal Shian would "call the Aquines" and the sea horses would herd fish into nets, whereupon the catch would be shared.

"So where are these Shian now?" asked Rana.

"Like the local humans, they found life harder and harder. That's why this place is so desolate. But I'm hoping the Aquines haven't forgotten this tradition."

The waves broke freely upon the shoreline as the loch met the open sea, and seabirds whirled overhead, their harsh cries mixing with the sound of the waves. Grandpa Sandy sat down by the water's edge and took out the phial of Aquine oil. Holding his sceptre over the water, he hit the surface several times, then reached over and poured out some of the oil.

"Ossian did that," blurted out Jack, "and the kelpie came up."

"Well, let's hope this is as successful." His grandfather smiled.

For a while, nothing happened. Jack scanned the water for any sign of the sea horses, then realised that he didn't know what they looked like.

"How big are they? The kelpie was huge. I only saw his head and neck, but that was several feet long."

"Big enough," mused Grandpa Sandy. "I should warn you that they can be frisky. If we're lucky, they'll take us down the coast. But be prepared to get wet."

"Have you done a lot of this, then?" enquired Rana.

"Not since I was a boy."

Rana looked at Jack and pulled her eyes wide open. *That wasn't yesterday!*

They waited for what seemed like hours. Bored, Jack wandered back along the shoreline. Grandpa Sandy had beaten the sea several times and had poured out some oil each time. There was just a dribble left in the phial.

Without warning, a pointed nose poked out from the water. Rana gave a startled yelp as a pair of beady eyes fixed on her. Jack came racing back from his dawdle.

Getting unsteadily to his feet, Grandpa Sandy began to stutter something. There was a silence.

"What did you say to it?" hissed Jack out of the corner of his mouth.

"I can't remember all the words," whispered his grandfather. "It's many years since I tried this."

The Aquine's head disappeared, and for a while nothing happened. Then it reappeared and was joined by another, and then two more heads, then two more again. The six heads were indeed horse-like, with what looked almost like a mane of scaly hair. The first one made a series of clicking noises, following which Grandpa again tried to remember the right sounds. He stumbled over phrases, repeating himself more than once, but they seemed to have the desired effect. The three largest of the Aquines rose further out of the water, revealing their dorsal fins.

"Come on."

Grandpa tucked his sceptre in his cloak, waded into the water and, clutching his walking stick firmly in his right hand, clambered onto the largest creature's back. Jack and Rana looked at each other, initially uncertain of what to do. Jack shrugged, then began to wade out.

"It's freezing!" He shuddered as the water reached his thighs.

Rana was only momentarily put off. She too strode out into the water and, like Jack, climbed on one of the Aquine's backs.

"Hold on tight," yelled Grandpa, gripping a fin as the creature set off.

The Aquines seemed to be letting them get used to the ride, because after a few moments at a gentle pace they began to speed up. Jack, Rana and their grandfather sat, their legs astride these strange creatures, eyes squinting against the wind and the sea spray. Jack's Aquine in particular seemed to like rising up on waves before splashing down again. Jack's teeth were chattering, but at the same time it was the most exhilarating ride of his life.

"This is even better than the horses when we went to France," shouted Rana, clearly in her element.

It *was* similar: horse-like creatures, moving faster than any Shian could hope to travel on their own – the low road excepted. But there was so much spray that Jack's clothes were quickly soaked, and a fine salt crust covered his face. He quickly gave up trying to lick his lips.

The three Aquines, together with their outriders, were a hundred yards or so out to sea, hugging the coastline. Every now and then Jack caught sight of a small sailing boat, and once even a human windsurfer. He looked across at his grandfather, who seemed to need all his strength and concentration just to keep his grip.

The sky darkened and a light rain fell. Rana complained: this was ruining a good ride, but Jack relished the fresh water on his face. However, as the rain intensified, the wind grew colder and the Aquines seemed to take a perverse pleasure in skimming just below the surface, allowing the sea to reach up to chest height. Jack was horrified to see Rana's Aquine sink below the waves, taking her with it for a full half-minute. When she surfaced again she gave a loud whoop.

"Whoo hoo! That was brilliant!"

She always boasts she can hold her breath for ages, thought Jack as he shivered. *I just want to get to this island.*

He was mightily relieved when he saw his grandfather point his walking stick at an island ahead of them.

They began to slow down. The Aquines cruised along the rocky coastline for a while, before slowing right down as a sheltered bay came into view. Reaching the shallows, Grandpa Sandy clambered off his Aquine. Jack and Rana followed suit, and together they waded ashore.

Jack was shivering as he collapsed cold, wet and tired on the shingle beach. He barely noticed stretching up to human height.

Grandpa Sandy turned around and waved his arm at the Aquines, which suddenly looked a lot smaller. He made some clicking sounds, then concluded, "*Tappa, Aquinas.*"

The Aquines clicked a response and disappeared back into the water.

"You remembered how to speak to them," pointed out Rana.

"It came back to me on the journey," her grandfather replied happily. "That brought back happy memories. But it didn't use to be so sore, crouching like that for a long time."

"I'm cold." Jack shivered. "Can we find some shelter?"

"We need somewhere we can get warm and dry." Grandpa Sandy seemed drained by the journey, and he hobbled up the beach.

Racing ahead, Jack found a cave entrance above the high-water line. He ducked inside and emerged quickly.

"It's dry in here," he announced. "I'll get some firewood. Rana, you go and look for a stream."

"What am I going to put the water in?" she demanded.

"The humans think of everything," said Grandpa Sandy, wheezing after his effort. "Look, there's some plastic bottles on the beach. Give them a good rinse, and we can use them."

Rana pulled a *yeuch* face, but did as she was told. The rain had gone off; Jack quickly found some driftwood and started a fire in the mouth of cave. The wood was damp and slow to ignite; it smoked horribly. To his surprise, Jack saw his grandfather return with three small rabbits and a brace of trout.

"How'd you get them?"

"A little crude, I suppose. I wanted to check my sceptre still worked all right after our sea journey. Not very neat, I'm afraid."

Jack saw the singe marks on each of the creatures, but was far too hungry to worry about blemishes like that. By the time Rana had returned with three plastic bottles filled with clear stream water, Jack had deftly skinned and skewered the rabbits, along with the fish, and placed them over the fire. They sizzled satisfyingly, and the smell of cooking wafted around the cave entrance. Stretching out the clean clothes they had brought so that they would dry first, they spread their cloaks and coats to one side of the fire, where they steamed gently. The three huddled around the flames and devoured the food. Grandpa seemed very old again.

There was no shortage of deadwood on the beach, and Jack replenished the fire every now and then. Their clothes dried slowly, and as they were lounging by the fire and digesting their meal, Rana arranged a series of pebbles around a circle she had drawn in the sand.

"Is that a clock?" asked Grandpa Sandy idly.

Rana pointed to an area to the right of the cave.

"I'm just copying that pattern there," she said casually.

Jack looked over to where Rana was pointing. His sense of ease and well-being evaporated instantly.

Twelve small twigs poking up from the sand formed a perfect circle some three feet in diameter.

Instinctively, Jack's hand reached into his pocket and grasped the yucca fibres. The oil was oozing out of it.

19
Marco Leo

"What's the matter, Jack?"

His grandfather's voice showed tiredness, but no hint of unease.

Jack's lips moved, but his mouth was parched and no sound came out. He stared hard at the ring of twigs. Grandpa Sandy's gaze followed Jack's, but there was no recognition on his face. Rana, sensing that something was wrong, had fallen silent.

Jack got uneasily to his feet, his damp clothes clinging to him. He gripped the yucca ring in his right pocket. There was no doubt about it: his hand was sticky.

"Shape-shifter," he mumbled.

"Where?" whispered Rana, following Jack's gaze. "I just thought someone had tried to make a sundial."

"Probably human children playing," said Grandpa, getting up and hobbling towards the twig ring.

"No, Grandpa!" blurted Jack, but it was too late.

Grandpa Sandy was knocked sideways as he stepped into the ring. Jack saw little more than a blur, but the roar that accompanied it would stay in his mind for a very long time, and Rana's scream would run that sound a very close second.

Jack's mind raced. What had Finbogie taught him? Get out of there. But he couldn't: his grandfather was lying on the ground, stunned; Rana was close to hysteria; and an enormous lion had appeared. The creature stood over Grandpa Sandy, but looked directly at the two youngsters. It roared again.

Jomo bag ... No, no good ... never got round to filling it with dirt ... Must stop it killing Grandpa.

The lion took a pace towards Jack and Rana as they cowered just outside the cave. Jack reached quickly into the Sintura belt around his waist, and felt around frantically for the hair wristlet Freya had given him. His heart thumped in his chest. Had he lost it? Would it work after being in the sea? Finally his fingers touched the hair bracelet, and he withdrew it quickly and slipped it onto his wrist.

"Felavert!"

The lion halted: it looked like it was trying to move, but couldn't.

Now what? thought Jack. *Now I'm supposed to get out of here; but I still can't. Grandpa's sceptre is in his cloak, and he's not even moving. At least Rana's stopped screaming.*

The lion tried to move forwards again, but its legs would not cooperate, and it stumbled to its knees.

And then the mist in Jack's head cleared. Just as he had with Konan the treeman, he thrust his right palm out towards the lion and shouted, *"Gosol!"*

There was a loud crack and a puff of smoke. When it had cleared, the lion had gone, and before Jack and Rana sat an old man clutching an ancient leather-bound book. He got to his feet and brushed himself down. Jack was so taken aback that he had no idea what his next move should be, but the old man took the initiative.

"Your heart is true, young man," he said, a kindly smile in his eyes. "You use that power well. Come, let us see what has happened to your grandfather."

"You nearly killed him," shouted Rana.

The old man looked steadily at her. "I believe he fell," he answered in an injured tone.

Grandpa Sandy had regained consciousness and was sitting rubbing the side of his head.

"Blasted stone," he muttered.

Then, looking up and seeing Jack and Rana with the stranger, he got to his feet, but the effort was too much, and he sat down again.

"I am afraid that your sudden appearance made me stumble," he said slowly. "That rock—" he indicated a stone partly covered with sand "—caught me on the temple." He rubbed slowly at a large graze on the side of his head.

"Let's have a look at that," said the stranger, kneeling down to examine Grandpa Sandy's head and placing the leather book on the ground.

Having inspected the graze and looked in Grandpa Sandy's eyes, he pronounced, "We should get you to lie down for a while. My house is not far. You'll be safe there."

Jack was looking quizzically at the leather-bound book on the ground.

I'm sure I've seen it before somewhere. But where?

He stooped to pick it up, but the old man beat him to it.

"I'll take care of that," he said firmly. "Follow me."

The path led them towards an old ruined cottage. Just one storey high, it had no roof and only two and a half walls.

"Is that his house?" hissed Rana to Jack. "There's hardly any of it left."

The old man stepped up to what had once been the front doorway, tapped a weather-beaten symbol carved into the stone lintel, and stepped through. Jack ushered his grandfather in next. Stepping over the portal, they entered a brightly lit, well-furnished room. Wooden beams held up the ceiling, the walls were adorned with pictures, and shelves were crammed with books. Rana entered last and let out a yelp of surprise as she caught sight of the room's interior.

The old man guided Grandpa Sandy over to a sofa and made him lie down. Disappearing into the next room for a minute, he returned with a bowl of water and a clean cloth.

"I can do that," announced Rana, glad to have something to do. She took the damp cloth and gently washed the graze on her grandfather's head.

The old man indicated to Jack that he should sit down, and Jack did so, gratefully. Jack's mind was racing. This didn't seem real, and yet he was sitting on what felt like a real chair. The outdoor sounds of wind and sea had died down to almost nothing, and a fire crackled in the grate.

"Please, can I ask who you are?" he managed.

"I am Marco." The old man's tone was even.

"We heard you were a cat. I didn't realise you were a shape-shifter."

"I have been many things. My lion is how some people know me."

"And please," Jack continued, "your book. It's like Matthew's. D'you know him?"

"My brother," replied Marco. Then, seeing the look of puzzlement on Jack's face, he continued, "Not my blood brother. We are four of many who echo the word." He leant forward and showed Jack the front of the book. In very faint letters Jack could just make out the word "Gosol" on the cover.

"You have the power of Gosol?" asked Jack breathlessly.

Grandpa Sandy tried to sit up at the sound of the word.

"We teach it. And you have clearly learned it, for you used it just now."

"I was taught that Gosol was the key to three treasures linked to the creator force," said Jack excitedly, "and that it has to do with believing in what's right."

"And acting on that belief lets in the light," added Marco. "Gosol will let light in, even through the tiniest crack. You'd be amazed what it can do."

"My grandfather taught me some of that . . . And there was someone else – but she's dead," added Jack.

"One of our followers, I know." Marco sounded sorrowful.

"You knew Tamlina?" asked Rana. "How?"

"I have been around for a long time," replied Marco. "I travel, and I teach. She came to us late, but she learnt well."

"A Brashat told us you were here," said Jack. "He didn't want to, but I made him. I'm looking for my father."

And with that, Jack told Marco the story of his father and Konan, and their imprisonment by the Grey; and how Konan had managed to escape, though his father was still suspended somewhere. He talked of how they had recovered the King's Chalice the previous year, after a battle with the Brashat, when the longship warriors and the monks had sailed through the forest. Marco smiled as Jack related the story of Comgall the monk and his leniency when the Brashat leader Briannan was defeated. Jack told of how the Kildashie had moved from their islands far out in the western ocean and had now overrun the Shian square in Edinburgh.

"And now you seek the Sphere to help you recover your homes?" Marco concluded Jack's tale.

"And find my father," added Jack quietly. "The two are together, I'm sure of it: where we find one, we find the other."

"And finish off the Kildashie — they're bad," added Rana. "It always got really cold when they were around. Like a winter that didn't stop."

Marco pondered for a moment.

"We had heard rumours of *infama* happenings on the mainland. It appears that they were true."

Grandpa Sandy had been lying silently on the sofa, listening intently. Now his head rolled to one side, and his reeking arm steamed gently.

That smells foul!

"I fear that knock to your grandfather's head has done more harm than we realised," announced Marco. "I will summon my brother Luka: he is a physician and will know what to do."

With that, he stood up and moved to the front door. Tapping the stone lintel again, he muttered under his breath.

"*Luka, referfrat.*"

Marco walked silently back to the sofa and knelt down. Eyes closed, he muttered inaudibly, then paused.

"Your grandfather has been ill already, I fear."

"Malevola poisoned him with a Phosphan curse," explained Jack. "Armina took care of him, and he'd almost recovered."

"Is he going to be all right?" enquired Rana anxiously.

"We may need to summon Armina as well. These illnesses may not be within Luka's knowledge."

"We tried to get back to Keldy: that's where the rest of our family are," stated Jack. "But the low road was sabotaged, we couldn't use it."

"It is some time since we used the low road here," said Marco thoughtfully. "I fear it will not be any use if the rest of the network is damaged."

"Couldn't we try it anyway?" asked Rana plaintively. "I want to see my mum and dad."

"The most pressing matter is to ensure your grandfather is all right," stated Marco emphatically. Then, relaxing, he continued, "But I'm sure we can see if the low road can be made to work."

Jack and Rana looked at each other. For several minutes, nobody spoke. Jack looked over at his grandfather. *He looks like he's sleeping*, thought Jack. *So peaceful*.

"Marco," began Rana, "where are we?"

"You're on Ilanbeg, by Loch na Keal."

"But why would Konan send us here?" demanded Jack. "I asked him where my father was, and Gosol made him reply. Is my father on this island?"

Marco looked thoughtfully at the youngster.

"You have courage; something tells me that you do not fear much. But you should respect real danger." Seeing the look of incomprehension on Jack's face, he continued, "Your father is not on this island, young man. But there may be ways to find him, if you prove yourself worthy."

"He's alive then?" Jack's voice rose as excitement and trepidation welled up inside him. "If he can be found, I'll find him. Where is he?"

"First, you must prove yourself. And the time for that has not yet come. But we can make preparations, so that we are ready."

Jack thumped the chair in exasperation. "But when's that?"

"When the moon rises after midsummer."

"That's a month away!" exclaimed Rana.

"We have plenty we can do in the meantime," answered Marco evenly. "I believe there is some more firewood outside, if you would be so good as to fetch it."

Jack stood up nervously. "I . . . I'm sorry I shouted," he mumbled. "I just want to find my father."

He moved uncomfortably towards the front door. Passing through, he glanced back at the room and saw the walls and the furnishings disappear. True to Marco's word, there was an untidy stack of kindling and small logs at the side of the house. Grasping several pieces, Jack went back through the front door. As he did so, the room materialised again.

"It keeps unwanted visitors away," said Marco, who had been watching Jack closely.

Jack set the logs down by the fireplace and arranged a couple on top of the dying fire.

"I hope you like fishing, because you can get some practice in," stated Marco.

"I'm good at fishing," announced Rana cheerily. "We do it all the time in Rangie."

"Not sea fishing, then?" asked Marco kindly.

Rana looked at Marco. "Is it very different?"

"Certainly. But you can show me what you know tomorrow. And now, I think we can eat a little."

Grandpa Sandy had not woken up by the time supper was finished. Rana, unsure whether this was a good sign or not, indicated to Marco that she would sit with her grandfather until he woke up.

"That may be a long wait, young lady." Marco's tone was even. "Luka will be here tonight; he will know what to do. You can dry your clothes by the fire."

Jack and Rana climbed upstairs to a small, furnished twin bedroom and settled down to sleep. So much had happened in the last couple of days. Attacks and unplanned journeys, Dunters and Aquines. But it was disconcerting that Grandpa was unwell again.

"D'you trust Marco?" asked Rana, snuggling down under the bedclothes.

"I think so. He seems kind."

"But he's a lion; couldn't he be dangerous?"

"His book is like Matthew's: didn't you notice? It has 'Gosol' on the cover. He must be all right."

"If he's got that much power, why can't he wake Grandpa up?"

"Perhaps the bump on the head started up the Phosphan curse again."

"Maybe. I thought he was just resting."

A steady rain pattered against the windowpane, and a low murmur from outside heralded a rising wind.

"Did you see that little wooden wheel on the wall?" asked Jack. "It's like the one the Blue Hag had when she was clearing the snows. It shows the seasons."

"I wasn't there, silly," said Rana sleepily. Then, after a pause, "It's funny being on an island, isn't it? It feels safe here."

Jack lay and thought about how much better it would be if Petros and the others were here too.

But at least I'm getting closer to my father. Even if I don't know where he is, I'm sure I'm getting closer.

20
Refugees

Jack slept soundly, dreamlessly, oblivious to the wild storm that raged throughout the night. When he finally awoke, the sun was streaming through the small window. Rana's slow, heavy respirations signalled that she was still fast asleep.

With a jolt, Jack remembered his grandfather. Dressing hurriedly, he clambered downstairs, but stopped in his tracks as he entered the front room. An old man sat by the sofa. Wisps of white hair fringed the back of his head, and a short, straggly beard fell from his chin. He appeared to be sleeping. Jack saw that his grandfather remained stretched out on the sofa, and he crept cautiously forward. A loud creak from a floorboard caused the man in the chair to stir. Opening his eyes, he looked first at Grandpa Sandy, then up at Jack. He smiled.

"Your grandfather is still sleeping. Would you like some breakfast?"

Nonplussed, Jack was grateful when Marco entered.

"I see you've met my brother Luka," announced Marco. "Do not be afraid; he is a physician and will take care of your grandfather."

Jack sat down at the table, where breakfast had been laid out.

"Is Grandpa all right?" he mumbled.

"I fear he has encountered many troubles," answered Luka. "Phosphan weakens the body and lingers long. Yesterday's concussion has not helped."

"When will he wake up?"

"When the time is right." Luka smiled again and looked over to the wooden wheel on the wall. "His troubles are far greater than yesterday's accident. Did you meet any evil creatures on your journey?"

"A Dunter in Dunvik threw some blood at Grandpa. The blood made his arm stink – like a burn. I got rid of the Dunter," added Jack. "Finbogie taught me how."

"We could do with the help of such people," mused Luka. "Treating Shian curses is not my strong suit."

"You mean . . . you mean you're not Shian?" Jack's voice quavered.

"We have been around for many years, but no, we are not Shian. Haven't you noticed? You're human-sized here." Luka spoke evenly, his voice reassuring. "We can do much, but there are limits to our powers. We are not magicians."

"But you're a physician," blurted out Jack. "You must know how to heal him."

"The greatest healer is time, my friend. Patience, mixed with knowledge and belief."

"So what can we do then?" asked Jack plaintively.

"We wait. And we will try to arrange for your friends Armina and Finbogie to come here."

"That may be difficult," pointed out Marco. "The low road is accessible here, but not on the mainland."

"So we're stuck here, then?" Rana had crept downstairs and had been listening from the doorway.

"The damage to the low roads is extensive – I have checked. That suggests an organised enemy. But it is not the work of the Kildashie."

"There was a Dunter and a demon with Malevola when she killed Tamlina," stated Jack. "And Grandpa told me about Boaban Shee last year. And there's always the Hobshee – not all of them got suspended."

"I see that you know a great deal about these things," said Marco with a smile. "That is useful. We will try to make contact with your family."

"They were going to Keldy," replied Jack. "We were supposed to go too, only we ended up in Dunvik."

"I gathered as much," said Luka. Then, seeing the look of surprise on Jack's face, he continued, "Your grandfather is quite alert when he is awake. But the concussion has revived previous troubles. It may be some weeks before he is fully recovered."

"Weeks!" exclaimed Rana. "He'd only just got over the Phosphan curse."

"The Phosphan has not completely left your grandfather; and I fear the Dunter's blood has made things worse," explained Luka patiently. "But when you have eaten, Marco will show you around."

After breakfast, Jack and Rana were shown the island. While small – only two or three miles long – there were many small coves and beaches that called out to be explored.

"I'll show you the best spots for fishing," announced Marco as he indicated one such inlet. "And there's someone you'll meet sometime. He's been here for many years, but he's a little nervous of strangers. There's a special fish that he's been trying to catch. Maybe you can help him to land it."

Jack and Rana explored the island over the next few days and quickly concluded that there weren't many parts that didn't have a sea view. Lengthening days and settled weather meant the peace of the island was undeniable. Time slipped by effortlessly.

It's so peaceful here, thought Jack as he sat and watched the sinking sun light up the clouds with a brilliant display of reds and oranges. *No trouble with Kildashie or Dunters . . . No more lessons with Murkle . . .*

Jack shook himself.

No, that's not why we're here. We're on a mission – kind of. Fishing's all very well, but we've more important things to do.

However, Luka's prediction about Grandpa's lengthy recovery proved to be accurate. The lazy pace of life did not change over the next few weeks, and so it was that Jack and Rana found themselves looking forward to the quietest midsummer either could remember.

Midsummer's day arrived without even a whimper. Despite detailed explanations from Jack and Rana, neither Marco nor Luka seemed inclined to celebrate the day. Even being shown the seasons wheel on the wall, which now indicated midsummer, did not seem to excite them. Grandpa Sandy did not seem concerned either, pointing out that it was hard to have a big celebration with only five people.

Jack returned to the house after a fruitless morning's fishing. He slumped moodily into a chair in the front room, swinging his empty satchel by his side.

"No joy, then?" enquired Grandpa Sandy kindly. There was a spark in his eyes once again as he watched his grandson. "Marco's got some good news. The low road's open again."

"You mean we can leave?"

"First we should find out how the rest of the family are. I've dispatched a grig to Keldy; we should hear back soon."

"I never understood how the low road could go under water," said Jack thoughtfully.

"The low road has its own rules. But it's interesting that Marco and Luka don't seem to use it."

"Marco said they *had* used it a while ago," said Jack. "But they're not Shian, Grandpa. Luka told us. This is an old human's house. And we're human size here."

"Indeed." Grandpa Sandy looked thoughtful. "That may explain some things I have been pondering. But I do believe that midsummer may prove to be significant." His eyes were smiling.

Jack thought back to the previous midsummer. All the excitement, the biggest festival in years, thousands of Shian from all over . . . and then the Brashat and their Hobshee thugs had spoiled it all. That had been the start of all the trouble.

Rana nearly exploded with excitement when she was told

the news. Arriving back at the house fish-less, her spirits soared at the thought of seeing her family again.

"Can we leave soon? I'll get my things."

Grandpa Sandy tried unsuccessfully to calm her down.

"We can go to Keldy, then work out how to get those Kildashie out of Edinburgh," she chattered happily. "And I can tell Lizzie about all the things we've done here."

"You will see your family soon enough." Standing by the doorway, Marco's face was set, serious.

"What's the matter?" quavered Rana.

"The grig has returned. Your family are only minutes behind her."

Grandpa Sandy stood up and walked over to Marco, taking him by the arm and leading him outside. Returning a few moments later, he announced, "Come along. We'll go and meet them as they arrive."

Jack and Rana followed him outside, unsure what to think. They quickly made their way towards the small copse that marked the low road entrance and had only a couple of minutes to wait before there was a whirr of activity.

Aunt Katie and Aunt Dorcas were first to arrive, both clutching Lizzie tightly. They stumbled off the mound, rising instantly to human height. Lizzie was crying and making retching noises. While Aunt Dorcas tried to console her, Rana ran and hugged her mother.

Within seconds, another whirring noise announced the arrival of Petros and Ossian. Jack's initial pleasure on seeing his cousins was halted when he saw that Fenrig and Morrigan were with them.

What's going on?

A further flurry of activity heralded a third group. Armina, tall and majestic, was holding hands with Uncle Hart, who had an angry weal across his closed eyes. All the new arrivals were dishevelled, their clothes dirty, their hair unwashed and tousled. All but Uncle Hart were clutching a bag of some sort, clothes and belongings picked up hurriedly as they'd left.

The scene was one of confusion. Relief, sadness and surprise mixed together. Jack cautiously approached Petros, but didn't know what to say. His cousin looked wretched. Fenrig and Morrigan retreated to the edge of the crowd, watching silently as puzzled embraces were exchanged. Grandpa Sandy walked up to Uncle Hart and hugged him, but his son seemed unable to respond. Grandpa Sandy looked fearfully at Armina.

"What has happened?"

"Keldy has been taken," she replied simply. "Hart is blinded – for now. Pierre is a prisoner of the Thanatos. They have colluded with the Kildashie and others. And it's like winter is back – the fields are frozen."

"But it's midsummer!" exclaimed Jack

"Dad's been captured," sobbed Lizzie. The journey's nausea had passed, leaving her free to dwell on her anguish.

"Who's taken him? And why?" demanded Rana.

"The Kildashie and the Dunters made a deal – an Unseelie alliance," explained Aunt Katie, trying to comfort her daughters, "and they brought in the Thanatos."

"Thanatos?" This was a new name to add to Jack's list.

"They're the condemned," gasped Uncle Hart, his eyes tightly closed. "They hover just this side of death. When they fight, they know they've nothing to lose."

"Why not? And why are they condemned?"

"If they're defeated, they know they're going to Sheol. Whatever they did in life, it was bad if that's their punishment."

Jack shuddered. Sheol: Shian hell, the worst fate imaginable.

"Why would they bother with the Kildashie?"

"The Kildashie have promised them the Chalice. The Thanatos think that it will keep them alive."

"And so they won't go to Sheol?"

Uncle Hart nodded. "We think so."

"But the Chalice doesn't work like that. It's not a magyck; it's about belief."

"These are desperate creatures, Jack. They'll try anything to avoid . . ."

"Dad tried to take 'em on," mumbled Petros. "But they move like lightning. One of them drew his sword across Uncle Hart's face."

Jack was overwhelmed. It was so good to see his cousins and the others again, but the news that things had got even worse was hard to take in. His uncle's face looked hideous.

In a daze, Jack led the bedraggled refugees back up to the house. When they arrived, Marco and Luka were standing by the door. They seemed unsurprised by the unkempt and distressed condition of the new arrivals. Holding up his hand for attention, Marco announced, "Luka will attend to your injuries. Our house is open to you all, but you see that it is not big enough for everyone."

"Grandpa can fix that," stated Rana.

"I'm afraid that Shian charms will not work on this house," replied Marco smilingly. "But it is midsummer, and I am sure that you younger ones will be happy to sleep out in tents. We have canvas enough."

"And you will be safe here, so do not fear." Luka spoke up now. "If matters are as serious as you say, then Marco and I will have work to do elsewhere, once I have seen to that man's eyes. You may stay here for as long as you need. Marco and I will leave the house to you."

"I saw Trog today," stated Marco. "He lives down on one of the bays. He was quite excited when I told him about you all. He believes the arrival of our young visitors – or one of them – is a matter of great fortune."

Jack looked quizzically at Marco.

"Trog?"

"It's not his real name. We call him that because he lives in a cave. When he arrived he was known as Erik Bloodaxe. He doesn't like his old name."

"How come Rana and I haven't met him before?"

"I haven't seen him myself since you arrived. He's practically a hermit, and shy of visitors, but something makes him think one of these young ones may be the answer to his prayers. In fact, Jack, I can take you to meet him now."

The house still looked like a ruin from the outside when he arrived back two hours later, but Jack hardly noticed. Filled with excitement, he could hardly wait to tell the others of Trog and his cave. As he approached the house, he saw that several small tents had been erected outside, but they were all unoccupied.

Stepping inside the house, Jack found everyone was crammed inside the now familiar interior. But his anticipation was dashed as he saw the look of defeat on the face of Petros, Rana ... well, everyone. Everyone, and Finbogie too, whose stern gaze met Jack's astonished look.

"Midsummer opened up the low road, Jack," said his defence tutor. "But it's done something else. You remember that Daid said he'd touched the Stone at Oestre? I've just come from Edinburgh, and midsummer's worked the same trick. If the Kildashie can work out how to get the Stone out, it's all over."

21
Trog

That was it, then. Hundreds of years of waiting to get the Stone back, and now the Unseelie had just walked uninvited into Edinburgh and midsummer had granted them the Stone. Just great. To say nothing of them turning midsummer back into winter.

Jack rounded on Marco and Luka, demanding, "Can't you take the Kildashie on?"

"Young man, you mistake our purpose here. My brothers and I are teachers; we do not interfere directly in the affairs of people. Or, at least, only rarely." Luka spoke calmly.

"But you have the powers of Gosol," Jack persisted. "And you've told us that we always have to fight for what's right. Isn't fighting evil part of what you do?"

"We *are* part of that fight," continued Luka. "But we operate through people – human or Shian. If they learn well from us, then they will know what to do. That is our commission."

"Well, tell us then: what do we do?" Jack shouted angrily.

Aunt Katie stood up and moved over to Jack, putting her arms around him. Her eyes were moist, but she looked firmly into his eyes.

"Jack, trust them. They're good men."

"But how?" Jack wanted to push his aunt away.

"We cannot give you all the answers." Marco spoke up now. "But we can show you how to find them. And I have already started that. Perhaps you ought to tell the others what you have learnt this afternoon."

"Well . . . we went to see Trog. He's not that old . . . I mean, he doesn't look all that old. He's a warrior-something . . ." Jack broke off.

"Warrior-savant," interjected Marco.

"Yes. He used to be a warrior, now he spends his time seeking wisdom. His cave is tucked away; you hardly notice it. Rana and I have been here a month, and we've never even seen him. For seven years he's been trying to catch this big fish. It's something to do with finding wisdom, or good luck . . ." Jack's voice trailed off.

"Trog is a warrior who came here with the Norse invaders." Marco took over. "But he's no ghost, like the ones you saw last year. He was left for dead, but his body had fallen by a well whose waters have powers that stop ageing. But once taken, that person cannot leave. They must return to drink the waters of the well every full moon, or their body will wither and die, and their soul with it."

"You mean he just drinks from the well and he'll live forever?" Rana sounded incredulous. "Then why doesn't everyone go there?"

"His long years come at a price," stated Luka. "He is slowly atoning for his bloodlust, but the anger can flare quickly. He needs wisdom if he is to have a peaceful death. To get that wisdom, he believes he must catch and eat the swordfish of fortune."

"It's this enormous fish," blurted out Jack. "The first person to taste its flesh will be shown where the *Mapa Mundi*'s hidden. It's a map that shows its owner where his heart's treasure lies. Trog believes it will lead him to a peaceful death."

"The manuscripts said that about the Sphere." Grandpa Sandy's voice was weak. "The third treasure."

"But a map's not round," pointed out Jack.

"Globe maps are," asserted his grandfather. "And if this one shows the right path to follow, that must help us."

"We can get the Stone back and get rid of the Kildashie." Rana sounded triumphant.

"But we don't know that this one's the Sphere," stated Petros. "Jack just said it was a map."

Jack looked round at his cousin, and as he did so he became acutely aware that Fenrig and Morrigan had been in the corner of the room all this time. Marco intercepted his gaze and guessed his thoughts.

"Certain treasures are there for all, young man. The map may be owned by anyone whose heart is true."

Well, that rules Fenrig out.

Marco handed Jack a book from the shelf, an old tattered volume with indistinct script on the cover. Opening it, Jack found these words on the first page:

Mapa Mundi, map of the world,

Shows oceans, lands, a flag unfurled,

But he who would know every part,
Inside the Sphere will see his heart.

"So the map is a sphere," said Jack triumphantly. "And to get it we have to find this swordfish."

"But if Trog ... or whatever his name is ... has been searching for this magic fish for years, he won't like it if someone else catches it," announced Finbogie.

"Trog does not own the fish, but he has made it his task to catch it, and out of respect, I would not expect any of you to steal it from him. Tomorrow we will take some of the other youngsters to meet him. Perhaps, in time, the others too."

As the meeting broke up and the youngsters prepared to bed down in their tents, Jack saw Fenrig and Morrigan in deep discussion. Fenrig stared briefly at Jack at one stage, but said nothing.

The next morning, Marco took the youngsters to see Trog. Fenrig complained bitterly about not having slept all night; Jack had had no difficulty in getting to sleep on his bed sheet outside and was raring to go. He thought that Morrigan would remain with her brother, but she seemed to prefer Ossian's company. The two of them followed at a distance.

Rana and Lizzie led the way with Marco, chattering excitedly.

"I want to see the well where he drinks," proclaimed Lizzie. "Something that stops you growing old must be pretty special."

"But I want to get older," answered Rana. "At least, until I'm adult. I don't want to be stuck aged twelve."

"I must warn you not to drink from the Nanog well," stated Marco emphatically. "Or you will be doomed to remain here."

"The waters come from Nanog?" exclaimed Lizzie. "I thought it was just a tale."

"But a true tale," stated Marco, turning round to give the others the same warning. Jack and Petros were discussing fishing tips, while Fenrig followed on a little behind: listening, but never joining in.

Jack reached the shoreline within minutes, where the tide was out.

"You'd never come across it by accident," he said, pointing to the mouth of a cave well above the high-tide mark.

"You mean he really lives in a cave?" spluttered Fenrig with disgust. "I thought you were joking."

"He has chosen this life to atone for his past," explained Marco. "He lives simply, and he seeks wisdom and understanding. But I warn you: his past haunts him still."

Marco indicated to the youngsters to wait while he went to the cave. When he returned a few minutes later, he was followed by a man who looked no older than twenty. His fair shoulder-length hair fell over a ragged goatskin jacket, his face was weather-beaten, and a coarse beard tumbled down over his chest. A rough leather belt was tied around his waist, and he wore loose woollen leggings. His feet, leather-brown, were bare.

Jack approached, nodding hopefully, but there was no light of recognition in the man's eyes.

Petros looked enquiringly at Jack, who just shrugged.

"I don't think he remembers me, even from yesterday."

"This island is rarely visited by Shian," explained Marco

simply. "That's why you've stayed at human size here. In fact, it's so small, few humans visit it — there's nothing much here to see. But Trog has been here for over a thousand years; in that time he has seen a few people come and go. Play on the beach until he gets to recognise you all."

Jack and Petros sat where the edge of the beach met the small field and tried to work out whether the map was their true objective or a distraction.

"I can't see how a map is a sphere," stated Petros. "If it's flat, like maps are, then you couldn't make it into a round shape. It wouldn't fit."

"But if it's special," claimed Jack, raking his fingers through the mixed soil and sand, "then maybe it can do different things. Anyhow, what else are we going to do? If Edinburgh and Keldy have been captured, there's no point trying to go back there." Absent-mindedly, he stuffed a little of the soil–sand mixture into his jomo bag.

"Keldy's definitely taken," shuddered Petros. "I don't ever want to see Thanatos again. I thought the Kildashie were wild, and whatever they do to the weather is desperate, but they're kittens compared to the Thanatos. What they did to Uncle Hart . . . ugh!"

"What . . . what d'you think they'll do with your dad?"

Petros was silent for a while. He turned away from Jack and wiped his eyes.

"Mum thinks they'll kill him. Maybe not on purpose, but they're like savages." His nose sounded blocked.

"How many were there?"

"A few dozen, I guess. Enough, anyway. Even Uncle Hart couldn't stop them."

"So what happened to the others from the square?"

"People were all over the place," replied Petros. "I think Freya and Purdy got away though. Daid got Murkle out. He knew some human spaces that the Thanatos wouldn't get to."

"So Rob from Cos-Howe betrayed the Congress?"

"I think Ban-Eye was in on it too. But the Kildashie killed her anyway. And Atholmor. Finbogie says he's definitely dead."

They sat in silence, looking out over the bay's clear blue water.

"What d'you think of Trog, then?" asked Jack.

Petros shivered. "Totally uncivilised. Imagine living in a cave. Even the humans aren't that daft."

"The cave's brighter than you'd think," replied Jack. "And he's all right too. He doesn't say much, but he lit up when he got talking about this swordfish. He thinks it's his escape from here."

"I didn't understand that," said Petros. "If you eat this fish, suddenly you know things?"

"You know what you need to know. For him, it's getting the Sphere."

"And he thinks that'll help him die?"

"Die peacefully; he's still troubled by what he did way back."

Their conversation was interrupted by Marco, who had approached quietly.

"Trog feels ready to meet you all now, one at a time."

Jack was first to his feet, and he made his way up towards the mouth of the cave where Trog sat, a little apprehensively. In turn, the seven youngsters approached and chatted for a while. When they had all done so, Marco indicated that they should return to the house, explaining that he and Luka would have to leave the next evening.

"We must go to the mainland. But you young ones can come back here tomorrow morning. Trog wants you to have a race on the beach."

"I'm fast," announced Rana emphatically. "I can beat Lizzie easily."

Jack looked at Fenrig, who just scowled back. Ossian and Morrigan, holding hands, appeared not to have heard.

"What's the race for?" asked Jack.

"To see who gets to help Trog catch the swordfish of fortune."

22

The Swordfish of Fortune

The house, when they returned, had been made habitable for everyone. Aunt Dorcas was arranging some flowers in old jars, while Grandpa Sandy explained to Uncle Hart how the house, despite not being Shian, was charmed. The scar across Uncle Hart's face was still angry, and he was in obvious pain. Armina had made soothing poultices, but was complaining that everything was human-sized and not as she liked it.

Aunt Katie tried to put a brave face on when she heard the youngsters arrive.

"How was the beach? And Trog? Did he tell you anything useful?"

Rana and Lizzie began to relate excitedly what Trog's sheltered bay had been like. Jack decided to let them talk. He was trying to plan ahead for Trog's race. Jack could run quite fast, he knew that, but Ossian and Petros were bigger and stronger than he was, and Fenrig was no slouch.

The rest of the day was spent showing the new arrivals around. Ossian and Morrigan had returned much later and didn't seem to mind the scolding they got from Aunt Katie. Rana had taken Lizzie off, proclaiming that there were some things only girls should know about. As Jack gave Petros a tour of the island, Fenrig tagged along, always a little behind.

The next morning, Ossian made good his escape before breakfast was over. Aunt Dorcas and Armina were busy tending to Uncle Hart's eyes and didn't notice as the young man slipped silently out of the house. Morrigan disappeared soon after, and the two were not seen again all day.

Jack led Petros, Rana and Lizzie off back to Trog's bay. Fenrig, as tight-lipped as ever, followed on behind. When they got there, they found that Trog was waiting. He wore a bow over his shoulder and carried a quiver of arrows.

"The others are not here?" Trog spoke in a quiet voice.

Jack looked at Petros, then at Fenrig. "I don't think they're coming. They're . . . busy."

Fenrig's snort of disgust needed no translation.

"When are we racing, then?" demanded Rana.

"You must first understand what the race is for." Trog spoke earnestly.

"Marco said: to help you catch the swordfish," stated Lizzie.

"But do you know why the fish is special?"

"Eating it will show you the *Mapa Mundi*," continued Lizzie.

"But to use the map, your heart must be pure, and true," replied Trog patiently. "That is why I fear I may never find it."

There was an awkward silence.

"Marco said you'd been trying . . . to catch this fish for a long time," said Jack, falteringly.

Trog looked sadly at him.

"I have been here many years. I'm sure Marco has told you the reason I came. And why I never left."

"So why is this fish so hard to catch?" asked Lizzie.

"He's big, and wise. But I know the tides he likes at the midsummer full moon, and the pools where he hides. I sense he is near today."

"Marco said you thought that our arrival was a stroke of luck," chimed in Rana.

Trog looked hard at her.

"For seven years I have tracked this fish. I recently dreamt that a Shian youth would come and help me catch it."

"And eating it tells you where to find the map?" Fenrig spoke up now.

Jack eyed him suspiciously. *There's no way I'm letting him get the fish, or the map.*

"Is the race along the beach, then?" asked Lizzie, trying to steer the subject back.

"The main stretch around the rocks is half a mile long."

Fenrig was first to his feet, swiftly followed by Rana and Lizzie. Jack and Petros exchanged glances.

"Anything to get off this island." Petros' terror of the day before had gone.

The tide was coming in, and the youngsters had to clamber over the rocks to get to the beach. Trog explained that a flaming arrow, fired by him at the far end, would start the race.

Like the girls, Jack had decided that beach running was easier in bare feet. Fenrig, retying his laces, looked scornfully at him.

Rana and Lizzie started playing in the incoming tide, while

Fenrig practised stretching exercises. Jack and Petros kept an eye on Trog's progress, keen not to miss the signal when it came, but after a while it was hard to tell if he was still moving or not. It took him ten minutes to reach the rocks where the beach ended.

After what seemed like ages, the flame shot skywards.

Fenrig got the best start, having stolen a few yards while the others watched the end of the beach. He was fast, there was no doubt about it, and Rana put in a good bid, catching him up within a hundred yards. But, unable to maintain this sprint, she soon fell away, joining Lizzie, who was jogging along in last place. Petros fared better, slowly pegging Fenrig back until at last he overtook him. As Petros' lead stretched to five, ten yards, Fenrig uttered a shrill cry and fired a hex at his opponent's back.

"*Cadolex!*"

Petros staggered and fell, sprawling in the sand.

"Cheat!" shouted Jack, some ten yards back.

Spurred on, he sprinted and drew level with Fenrig as they came within a hundred yards of Trog. Edging just ahead, Jack sensed he had the beating of his old adversary, when Fenrig tripped over Jack's heels. They both stumbled, but while Fenrig fell, spraying sand up around him, Jack regained his footing and completed the race.

"Cheat!" yelled Fenrig, as he limped home. "You tripped me up!"

"How could I?" shouted Jack. "I was in front of you."

"It was an accident," said Trog calmly. "Unlike your hexing of the other lad." He looked sternly at Fenrig. "The prize can only be enjoyed by the one whose heart is true."

"Well, what does that mean?" scoffed Fenrig.

With a yell of rage, Trog drew a long steel knife from his belt and held it to Fenrig's throat. Fenrig, his eyes half closed in terror, whimpered.

"It's all right, Trog." Jack pulled Fenrig away, and the warrior-savant sagged. His arm dropped, but he continued to clutch his knife. He looked down at the sand, breathing heavily.

Petros and his sisters joined them now and berated Fenrig for his lack of sportsmanship. This change of focus allowed Trog to recover himself, and he said simply, "Jack will help search for the fish. The rest of you can stay here or go back to the house."

Fenrig stalked off. Rana announced that she and Lizzie would go back to Trog's bay for a while, as they liked the rock pools there.

"You'd better watch that tide," said Petros. "Look, I'll come with you. You'll be all right, Jack?"

Jack grinned broadly.

"I'll just get my shoes."

Jack jogged back along the beach with Petros and the girls. As they neared Trog's bay, Petros guided his sisters around the rocks, many of which were now underwater. Jack picked up his shoes and started to make his way back to where Trog sat gazing out to sea.

The sun was rising in a cloudless sky, and a warm sea breeze soon dried Jack's sweat. By the time he reached Trog, he was sticky and very thirsty.

"Can I get a drink?" he gasped.

Trog continued to gaze out over the clear blue water. Tiny

distant islands dotted the horizon; beyond them were thousands of miles of water.

Jack cleared his throat, unsure whether Trog had heard him.

"Can I have some water, please?"

As Trog handed Jack a water bottle, he looked at the youngster, searching his face.

"Are you ready for a battle?"

Jack swigged some water, then hesitated. Weren't they going fishing?

"I . . . I'm ready to catch the swordfish."

"I know every bay on this island; the tides and the winds are like my brothers. But this fish has eluded me for years."

"I . . . I meant I'm ready to help you."

Trog stood up, and without a word marched briskly off.

After half an hour they came to a small pebbly beach with rock cliffs to each side. The tide was nearly in.

"The retreating tide leaves rock pools." Trog pointed to where the rocks on the west side sloped down into the sea. "The moon is full tonight; the tide will be high. He likes to bask in the warm shallows."

Jack looked up at the cloudless sky. There was no doubt that the shallows would be warm today. But if the fish liked to swim there, how hard could it be to catch him?

"A rock pool sounds easy, doesn't it?" said Trog calmly. "But you've not seen this fish. He's special."

Jack's brow furrowed.

"A legend speaks of a large fish that spears men as if they were mackerel. This is him; I'm sure of it. Whoever eats this fish will be shown the *Mapa Mundi*. And I seek the wisdom that comes with it."

"Why's that so important?"

In response, Trog held his hands up and cradled Jack's head.

Instantly, a thousand sorrows flooded him. Grief, bitter heartache and every kind of distress poured into his very being. Misery and pain didn't come close to describing what he felt. Jack felt his head would burst, but it was his stomach that erupted, in a great wave of nausea.

Trog lowered his hands, and the feeling passed.

"That's what I have felt, day after day. And you wonder why I seek release?" Trog spoke softly. "The swordfish will give me that release. But he carries his own wisdom – he's too clever to strand himself in a rock pool. He is big and strong, too, even heavier than me. But his weakness is the midsummer full moon."

Jack squinted up at the clear blue sky. Though daylight, the full moon was clearly visible.

"I had a dream two moons ago that a Shian youth would help me catch him."

"So what do we do?"

"At high tide he'll bask in the shallows. There's a sand bank, where the entrance to the bay narrows. We'll get him there. But he's too wise to take bait and there's few nets would hold him. I can hit him with an arrow, but he'd make straight for the sea. That's why I need you."

"You mean I've to stop him?" asked Jack incredulously. "A monster with a sword for a nose?"

"In my dream the youth had some power I did not understand. You are Shian."

"I haven't got a sceptre," said Jack firmly, wondering if the race prize was that wonderful. "What can I do against a fish twice my size?"

"Only believe," replied Trog. "Have faith in your gifts."

Trog led Jack past the sandbank to the far side of the bay.

"When he rests there, you wade into the shallows. He'll grow sleepy in the warm water. When the time is right, I fire."

Jack could think of a hundred good reasons to go back to the house. Not getting speared by a monster fish was top of the list, but then he thought of the *Mapa Mundi*.

Without that, we can't find the Sphere, or my father, or get rid of the Kildashie.

Jack sat on a rock and waited. Twenty yards around the bay, Trog crouched and watched the shallow waters.

Waves lapped up the beach to where a line of seaweed revealed the high-tide mark. Nearly there.

The sun beat down on Jack's head, and he longed just to dip his head into the water. Trying to take his mind off the heat, he became absorbed in the attempts of a tiny crab to scale a rock, only to fall off repeatedly, washed away by the incoming tide. He didn't notice Trog stiffen, then stand slowly upright. It was some minutes before he was aware of Trog signalling to him.

Trog was pointing frantically at the water a dozen yards in front of him, but Jack saw nothing. The waves rippled against the rocks on which he sat, hunched down. Trog indicated to Jack to climb down into the water. Why?

Then Jack saw him. The dark purple back was almost invisible, but there ... a dorsal fin just poking above the surface.

Gradually, he edged his feet along the rock until he felt

sand under his toes, but every downwards movement caused ripples. The water was warm for the first foot or so, then cooler. Inch by inch, he crept away from the rock until he was halfway to the sandbank. The water was up to Jack's waist, the fish ten yards in front of him.

I don't know what I'm doing here. If that thing turns on me, I'm finished.

A sickly feeling gripped Jack's stomach, and his scalp tingled.

Trog had taken his bow from his shoulder and fitted an arrow, but he made no move to fire.

What's he waiting for?

It seemed like an eternity before Trog finally raised the bow and aimed down at the water. A pause.

Get on with it; this water's colder than it looks. Jack tried hard not to shiver.

Still no movement from Trog. Jack caught a glimpse of a silver blade projecting above the fish's mouth. He gulped.

Come on!

Twang!

The arrow met its mark; within two seconds Trog had repeated his fire. The great fish rose up, thrashing, then turned and made towards Jack.

Jack got a good look at the sword now: silver, three feet long, and about to kill him.

His mind flashed. Finbogie. Jack's blue eye blazed, and he raised his right wrist, pointing at the water.

"*Negladius!*"

There was a golden flash, and the great fish stalled, the two arrows rising from its back. Its momentum brought it towards

Jack, who stumbled, submerging himself as he tried to evade the sword. A great cry of triumph rose from Trog: he bounded forward into the water, splashing joyfully.

Jack stood up, dripping wet, and put his hand forward to stop the fish. It made no movement; tiny flurries of blood came from the two puncture wounds on its back.

"You did it!" cried Trog. "You believed!"

He reached Jack and embraced him. Then, turning, he tried to lift the fish out of the water. Realising that it was just too big, he pushed it back towards the beach. Jack clambered back onto the rocks and made his way round.

The tide continued to pulse forward onto the beach, its gentle surge carrying the great fish into the shallows.

"What a size! Six feet at least. And that sword – another three feet." Trog could barely contain his excitement.

Jack was still trying to piece together what he'd done. Then he realised. When he'd seen the sword, in a flash his mind had gone back to Finbogie's lessons ... how to disarm someone with a sword. He started to laugh.

Trog hauled the great fish onto the beach, well above the high-tide line.

"You didn't kill him; I should do him that honour now."

Trog reached into his waistband and drew out his long steel knife. Deftly, he drew the blade around the great fish's gills. Then he turned to Jack and knelt down.

"You have helped to release me. Do me the honour of eating this fish with me."

23
Revelation

Jack's mind raced. He had never seen such a fish – he'd never even known such monsters existed. Even at human size, Jack was dwarfed by it. And now it lay dead, its gills slit by Trog's steel knife.

Trog gazed at the swordfish, almost lovingly. He seemed at peace.

"I'll get some wood," said Jack, to break an uncomfortable silence.

He wandered to the top of the beach and began to scour for driftwood. Returning several minutes later with an armful, he found Trog just as he had left him.

He's almost in a trance.

Trog gave a start as Jack dropped the firewood. For a moment he looked unknowingly at Jack, then the light dawned in his eyes.

"Thank you." His voice was almost inaudible.

Jack looked away, embarrassed. "I'll get some more wood."

When he returned again, Trog had washed the sand from the swordfish's skin and lain the fish on some stones. Taking his knife from his waistband again, he quickly separated the beast's long sword from its body and skilfully whittled a handgrip at its base. Then, for good measure, he serrated the top half of the sword, giving it a sharp, jaggy edge. Brandishing the sword triumphantly, he declared, "For your help in conquering this magnificent creature, I award you this. I trust it will bring you good fortune some day."

Jack gratefully accepted the sword. It was a ferocious weapon that would be lethal in any fight. He cradled its sharp teeth in his arms.

"We'll prepare the fire, then the others can join us."

Trog placed the wood along the stones, creating a trench-like fireplace, and started a fire with a small piece of broken glass and some dried grass. This done, he skilfully gutted the fish and skewered the great beast's body with a long branch. Resting the skewer on larger rocks at either end of the trench, he sat back happily to watch the fish cook.

Jack marvelled at the speed with which the warrior had accomplished this task. However, he soon realised that the fish's size meant a very long cooking time, and he set off to look for more wood.

Initially, Trog seemed unhurried, revelling in his success, but after an hour he too realised that lunchtime was still some way off. He began to pace up and down the beach, finally announcing, "I must tell Marco. He will share in my good fortune. Will you mind the fish?"

Jack nodded.

"Don't eat it, though . . ." Trog's voice quavered, and he coughed.

"Of course not."

Trog set off, and Jack sat down to watch the fish and the fire.

It was a slow business. The enormous swordfish (minus its nose) hung six inches above the flames. Twice more, as the fire diminished, Jack fetched more wood. Gradually, he could see the fish start to cook properly. A delicious smell hung in the still air.

It could do with some seasoning; maybe Trog will ask Aunt Dorcas for some.

Trog had been gone a long time.

How much longer's he going to be?

The fish's flesh was browning nicely now, and the aroma was making Jack ravenous.

Still no sign of Trog.

Where's he got to?

Jack heard a sound behind him and, looking round, he saw a triumphant Trog leading all the others down to the beach.

"How's the cooking?" yelled Petros, still some way off.

Jack turned and inspected the fish. He noticed the flesh starting to bubble where one of the arrows had struck home. Without thinking, he pushed a finger against the raised blister.

Oww!

As his own skin burnt, Jack instinctively sucked his finger.

Silence. The sound of the sea had gone. Then a ringing of bells. And a blinding light.

Jack felt as if he was being lifted up bodily. The ringing in his ears continued, and he saw a dark shape in the middle of the brightness.

The dark shape got bigger – or was it moving towards him?

Bigger and bigger, and soon it blotted out the light. Jack panicked; he tried to scream, but no sound emerged.

The darkness engulfed him.

What is time? Jack had no notion of how long he was in the tunnel.

For a tunnel was where he was. After ages (a minute? An hour? A day?) he could see the end of the tunnel approaching. Speed slowed down.

There's light at the end of the tunnel; something's fluttering ... but there's a shape there. A man ... or something like a man ... covered in blood vessels ... He's got something in his hand ... He's ...

Jack felt a searing pain in his left shoulder.

Then a deep gasp, like he hadn't taken a breath in several minutes.

Uuuh.

"Are you all right, Jack?"

Aunt Katie was peering down at him.

Jack blinked. The pain in his shoulder eased, and he became aware of the others crowding around.

"What ... what is it?"

Luka bent down.

"Jack, something important has happened."

Jack sat up. Everyone was looking at him ... No, not everyone. Trog stood a little way off, pointedly facing away.

"You ate the fish, Jack."

Jack's heart raced. He hadn't eaten anything . . .

He looked around at the huge swordfish, still on its skewer.

"I . . . the skin was blistering . . . I touched it . . ."

And Jack realised.

He stood up and moved unsteadily over to Trog. The warrior refused to turn around.

"I . . . I'm sorry . . . I didn't mean to."

Marco tugged Jack's arm. "We'll leave him for a while."

"I didn't think . . ." Jack stopped, remembering how Trog had shown him the tormented sorrow he felt each day. That had been worse than anything he'd known, and the nausea returned, though he wasn't sick this time. As pressing as his own quest was, he couldn't bear to think of Trog enduring such torment any longer. "Could . . . couldn't you just go anyway?"

"It doesn't work that way, Jack. You had the vision." Marco led Jack away and motioned to Luka to follow.

"Tell me, Jack, what did you see?"

Jack looked at the two of them, uncertain what to reply.

"After the light," prompted Luka.

"It . . . it was like I was moving along a tunnel. As I got to the end, there was a light . . . Then a man appeared . . . At least, it was like a man . . ."

"And what did this creature do?"

"He had something in his right hand . . . and then I felt a pain." Jack touched his left shoulder, which bore no sign of any injury.

"Was there nothing else?"

"Some . . . something was behind him. It moved, like there was a wind."

"Like a flag?"

"The *Mapa Mundi*?" Jack almost jumped for joy; then he corrected himself. It had been an accident; he wasn't supposed to have eaten the fish. Had he cheated? If he had, then his heart couldn't be true.

Marco didn't speak, but led Jack back to where Trog sat disconsolately on the beach. The warrior looked drained, defeated. He looked up as they approached.

"You have taken my prize."

Jack shuffled his feet awkwardly.

"Maybe I should have realised that I would never reach it. But in my dream . . ."

"Perhaps Jack's need is even greater than yours," said Marco softly.

It was Trog's turn to remain silent.

"You can come too . . ." started Jack.

Marco led Jack away, leaving Luka with Trog. "Leave him be for now. We need to show you St Fingal's tunnel."

"Fingal's . . . Fin . . . St Fin! St Fin's cave, like in the manuscripts! You mean . . . you knew about the tunnel?" asked Jack incredulously.

"We had to be sure you were the one," replied Marco.

"The one?"

"The one to complete the challenge." Marco spoke evenly.

"But . . . Trog should've got it. You said yourself."

"You didn't steal it; and when you saw his pain, you even tried to give it to him. Your heart is true."

"Who was that at the end of the tunnel?"

"Not who: what. Something you must overcome. More I cannot say, but I believe you have the power to triumph."

Jack frowned. The creature at the tunnel end had looked like a man at first, but something now made him doubt this.

Luka rejoined the group and asked Aunt Dorcas to take over the cooking. The group sat around the fire and ate the swordfish, but for a while nobody spoke. Jack felt that everyone was staring at him, and eventually turned his back on the others, sitting gazing out over the water. The moon faded. Jack saw a V-formation of wild geese overhead, their plaintive honks just audible.

"Midsummer is not their usual time here; it is a sign." Luka had silently joined him. "They help each other. And you will need great help to achieve your goal. But I sense that you have this."

Jack shrugged his shoulders.

"You must choose who shall accompany you. Choose well."

Jack sat and thought. *Petros, obviously, and Ossian, if I can get him away from Morrigan. And Grandpa, if he feels well enough. What about the girls? And Finbogie? He could be useful if I'm up against some really evil Shian. Uncle Hart's blind, he can't help.*

"We must go soon," said Luka firmly. "The tunnel will only be visible for a brief time."

Jack stood up and went over to Petros.

"You'll come?"

Petros looked round and saw everyone looking at him. He gulped. " . . . OK."

Jack looked around, but couldn't see Ossian.

"He's gone off with Morrigan again," said Petros, reading Jack's mind.

"I'll ask Grandpa."

Luka was tapping his foot impatiently as Jack went to speak to his grandfather.

"Will you come, Grandpa? We need to get the map."

Grandpa Sandy was quickly on his feet, rejuvenated by the discovery that they were finally making progress.

"We must get there soon." Luka's voice was firm, and he set off towards the west, past Ilanbeg's only real wooded area.

Jack scurried after him, with Petros in hot pursuit. The others followed on, keen to see what would happen next.

In fifteen minutes, Luka had led them to a small hillock that overlooked a tiny inlet facing west.

"The tunnel will show itself when the time is right. Jack – follow your heart. Marco and I must leave for the mainland now."

"Where's the tunnel?" demanded Fenrig.

In all the commotion, Jack had completely forgotten about his tailoring colleague. But he wasn't going to let Fenrig share in anything now.

"Luka said I've to choose who's coming. I'm taking Petros and Grandpa."

"We'll see." Fenrig looked slyly at Jack.

Jack, Petros and Grandpa Sandy sat down to watch the tiny mound that Luka had indicated. It didn't look like much.

A cool breeze blew in from the Atlantic, and seagulls called raucously overhead.

Jack sat and cradled his sword. The memory of the haunted look on Trog's face troubled him.

But I didn't mean to eat the fish.

He felt the serrated edge and imagined how much damage this would cause if drawn across flesh.

"How will we know when the tunnel opens?" asked Petros.

"Somehow we're supposed to know," answered Grandpa Sandy. "But this island is not good for Shian charms. There's nothing here to make our powers work that well."

"Fenrig managed a hex when we had the race," pointed out Petros. "And Jack stunned the swordfish with a Negladius."

"Then it's me," said Grandpa Sandy gloomily.

A rabbit appeared on the hillock and hopped towards Jack. Jack eyed it curiously. Apart from fish, rabbits had been all there was to catch on Ilanbeg, but after his lunch, Jack wasn't hungry. The rabbit sat there a moment, then hopped back, disappearing down its hole.

A minute later, it repeated the performance.

"That hole's got bigger," said Jack, as the rabbit repeated this a second time.

"It's the tunnel," shouted Petros. "Come on."

They went over and examined the hole. It had indeed grown in size and was now some three feet in diameter.

"I hardly think I'll fit down there," stated Grandpa Sandy. "Not at human height."

"*We* can get in." Jack inspected the hole again. "Can't you shrink yourself, Grandpa?"

"It doesn't work. Whether it's me, or this island, the charms I'd normally use just don't work."

The rabbit's head appeared again and disappeared promptly.

"The hole's getting smaller!" shouted Jack.

Indeed, the tunnel entrance was slowly shrinking.

"Come on!" Jack grabbed his sword and scrambled head first into the hole. He slithered down a straight chute, dirt forcing its way into his mouth and eyes. He landed with a bump. It was pitch dark.

Petros was just a moment behind him. As he landed, he unblocked the chute and a shaft of light lit up a small clearing.

"Where are we?" spluttered Jack, rubbing the mud from his face.

There, in a shaft of light, was the rabbit. Surrounded by twelve tiny sticks.

24
The Mapa Mundi

Jack blinked, his heart pounding. In the half-light he couldn't quite believe what he was seeing. He tried to swallow, but his mouth was desert-dry. Reaching down into his Sintura belt, he searched frantically for his wristlet. His fingers found a myriad charms, but not the item he sought.

What was the word Finbogie had taught him? A rabbit . . . A rabbit has . . .

"You're thinking of 'Divisungulam'."

Jack rubbed his eyes. The rabbit had disappeared, and in its place was a tiny korrigan, sitting hunched in the twig circle. Its eyes were enormous for such a minute head, and its skin was pale, almost see-through.

"Yes, I'm a shape-shifter. I've been trying to get you to come down the tunnel for ages." Its voice was harsh.

Petros sat rigidly, his eyes like saucers.

"Will you show us the way?" asked Jack nervously.

"I can show you how to start. But I have no wish to meet . . ." The voice trailed off.

Unsure he wanted to know the answer, Jack asked, "What is that creature . . . at the end of the tunnel?"

"Something you won't want to meet a second time. It's the Nucklat. But if you are here, then you have been chosen."

Up to now, Petros hadn't uttered a sound. Now he tried to speak.

"What is it?" His voice was little more than a croak.

"A korrigan," whispered Jack. "We saw some at the festival last year. And at Cos-Howe."

"I smell fear on you," the tiny creature squeaked harshly to Petros. "The fear of a city dweller."

Petros shifted uncomfortably.

"We need to get to the *Mapa Mundi*," said Jack firmly. "My cousin is here to help."

"Then you will need more help. It's unusual . . . but I will leave the tunnel entrance open for others."

Jack looked at Petros, who shrugged.

"Grandpa can join us. We may need all the help we can get."

"That's true. Can you make it big enough for our grandpa?"

"I'll try. But it may take some time."

Jack moved over to the bottom of the chute and called up. "Grandpa! Can you hear us?"

A muffled shout came back. "I can't get down the hole."

"Come down when the hole gets bigger," shouted Jack.

"You need to go," the korrigan snapped. It stood up

and marched off down an unlit passage some three feet in height.

Jack placed his sword down his spine with its base wedged into his belt. He began to crawl after the korrigan.

"It's freezing," grumbled Petros, as he made to follow. "And it's bad enough staying at human size, but crawling in the dark's ridiculous."

Jack's scowl was lost on Petros in the almost complete darkness.

They had been crawling downhill for several minutes when Jack became aware of a glow ahead. The light got stronger, and eventually they emerged into another small clearing. Sticking out from the side walls were a staff and a sceptre, each with a small, brightly glowing crystal.

"We are at the edge of the sea," squeaked the korrigan. "The tunnel proper begins here."

Jack peered ahead. The tunnel at the other side of the clearing was much larger, fully six feet in height.

That's a relief.

"Can't you come any further?" asked Jack nervously.

The korrigan shook its head.

"Be on your guard – the Nucklat moves swiftly. I will go back and make sure the tunnel entrance remains open."

Without further word, the korrigan skipped off.

Jack looked at Petros. "Let's go."

"Wait a minute." Petros sounded anxious. "What are we getting into? We've no idea what the Nucklat's like."

Jack fingered his sword. "We have to. The *Mapa Mundi's* down there somewhere. When we get that, we'll know how to get rid of the Kildashie."

Petros shuffled his feet.

"But with more help we've got a better chance. It'll buy us time, anyway."

Time! Jack suddenly remembered the sand timer he'd picked up at Dunvik. Retrieving it from his Sintura belt, he squinted at it in the dim light. The sands were running through steadily.

"I'm sure this is telling us how much time we have left."

Jack grabbed the crystal-topped staff and motioned for Petros to take the sceptre from the wall. Together they set off along the taller tunnel. Jack shivered as they advanced downhill. It was definitely getting colder.

The crystals were bright, but they could only throw a gloomy light in the tall, dark tunnel. The boys' shadows flickered on the side walls as they walked. There was no sound, save their footsteps.

They had walked for a good hour when Jack felt the tunnel start to level out, then start uphill. Checking the timer, he saw that the sands were running through fast.

"It's uphill now; we'll need to speed up."

He started to jog, and Petros reluctantly followed.

"Can't we have a rest?" panted Petros after ten minutes.

"We've no time," said Jack firmly, and pressed on.

The slope got gradually steeper, and Jack felt himself start to sweat. A curious mixture of anticipation and fear filled him – running in the dark and not knowing what was just ahead made him want to slow down, and yet he knew that time was tight. Petros was as fit as Jack, but he hung back, reluctant to take the lead.

It was another half hour at least before Jack saw the light ahead. With a sickening sense, he realised that it was just as he had seen in his vision. He stopped.

"This is it. Whatever the Nucklat is, it's at the end of this tunnel."

Jack could hear the sea clearly now. Giving Petros his crystal staff, and taking the swordfish sword from his belt, he proceeded cautiously. Then he stopped and turned round.

"I heard something. Back there." Jack pointed back down the tunnel.

"There's nothing there. Let's get out of here."

The light grew stronger as they approached, but not as quickly as Jack remembered it from his vision. His mouth became dry and his chest felt tight. The sound of the sea grew stronger, a roaring swell.

Slowly, he edged towards the end of the tunnel.

Any minute now . . . it'll jump up at me.

But nothing came. Jack emerged from the edge of the tunnel and found himself on a rock path inside the mouth of a cave, and some ten feet above a surging tide. The cave's rock formation was curious – like hexagonal columns stacked together.

Petros emerged too, squinting in the light, and placed the staff by the cave wall. The youngsters were halfway back in a sea cave, with the open sea to their left. A sunset glow partially lit up the cave's interior. The curiously shaped rocks around them almost sang as the waves coursed in.

"There!" Jack shouted in triumph, pointing to the rear of the cave.

Sure enough, fluttering in the breeze, was an old flag that

seemed to hover unsupported. Its markings were indistinct . . .
two circles . . . each definitely looked like a map.

"The *Mapa M—*"

Jack got no further. With a great roar, the Nucklat emerged
from the sea below them. It had the head and body of a man
– *A skinless man! Urrgh . . . !* – but in place of its left arm were
several long tentacles. With a sweep of one of these it knocked
Petros against the cave wall. His head met rock with a
sickening thud, and he crumpled, motionless, his sceptre
spinning away onto the path.

Jack tried to step back, but there was no room. The Nucklat,
its bottom half still below the water, cut off any retreat down
the tunnel. It roared again, a deafening sound that resounded
through the cave.

Jack looked frantically, but the fallen sceptre was out of
reach. The Nucklat emerged further from the water, roaring
hideously . . . but it had no legs . . . only more tentacles. Jack
was so astonished he barely registered the trident in its right
hand. With a swift thrust, the trident found its mark.

Aargh!

Blood gushed from Jack's left shoulder. Almost crazily, he
searched his memory for anything Finbogie might have taught
him that would help. A fish . . . an octopus . . .

Nothing.

Then he looked at his right hand.

The swordfish!

Jack slashed at the approaching spear, deflecting it. Hacking
again, Jack sliced off the end of one of the Nucklat's huge
tentacles. With a roar, the beast fell back, its remaining tentacles
swirling around madly, blood and slime spurting from the

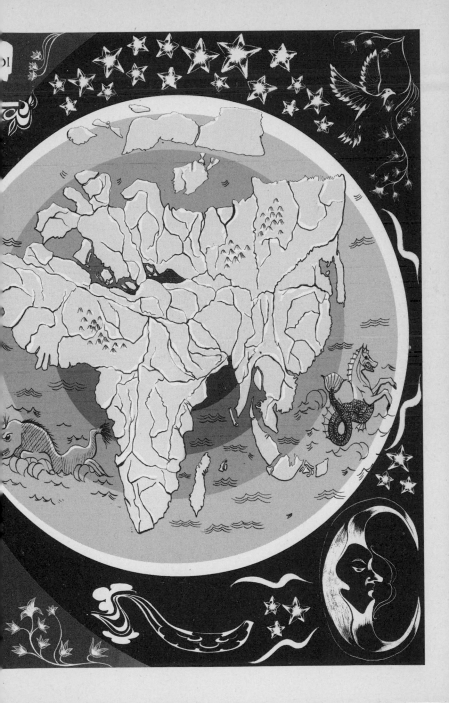

lacerated limb. Jack risked a quick look at the back of the cave and was astonished to see the map lowering itself. He had no time to react to this, for the Nucklat was on him again. Slashing furiously at the creature's flailing limbs, he continued to edge back towards the rear of the cave.

"It's Fenrig! He's stealing the map!"

Rana's panicked scream from the tunnel entrance surprised even the Nucklat, which paused in its pursuit of Jack and looked round to find the source of the noise. Jack looked round to the back of the cave again, and to his astonishment saw Fenrig smiling evilly back.

"Take a last look at the map," sneered the young Brashat, waving it tauntingly at Jack. With his back to the rock wall at the end of the path, he watched the scene in front of him with malevolent relish.

The Nucklat, perplexed at this appearance of yet another small creature, roared again and began to advance on Jack once more. A wave crashed into the cave, spraying Jack with salt water.

The timer! The sands will be through in a few seconds!

Re-energised, Jack whirled his sword again and once more succeeded in hacking off the end of a tentacle, but there were so many of them, and the creature, maddened with the pain, only seemed more menacing. A tentacle caught Jack around the ankle, and he fell against the rock wall.

"He's taking the flag!" Lizzie had appeared at the tunnel entrance now. She grabbed the staff Petros had set down by the the cave wall and swiped at the Nucklat's body.

The Nucklat, its attention diverted once more, turned to identify this new arrival. Jack seized his chance. Grabbing his sword, he scrambled to his feet and slashed the great creature across its eyes. The serrated edge raked agonisingly over flesh; blood and gloop gushed out, and the Nucklat fell back, roaring in agony. Then, lunging blindly forward, its tentacles thrashed against the rock wall, instinctively clutching onto Fenrig's leg as he prepared to make his way along the path. Squealing in surprise and pain, the young Brashat was lifted up in the air. The map flew from his hand, fluttering as it drifted back to the cave floor.

"Here, Jack!"

Rana scrambled to the sceptre and flipped it up. Catching it, Jack aimed it at the great sea creature, which was sinking down into the water, dragging a screaming Fenrig with it.

"*Gosol!*"

There was a flash in the gloom of the cave, and as the creature arched up into the air, it wrapped a second tentacle around Fenrig's upper body.

Fenrig tried to scream, but the Nucklat's primeval grip ensured no air could get in or out.

"It's going to kill him!" screamed Lizzie.

Jack paused for a half-second. Did his old adversary deserve to be rescued?

He didn't really have to think about the answer. Jack kept his arm trained on the creature, and the glow that had shot from the sceptre remained fixed on the Nucklat's slowly pulsating body. Over the next minute its grip lessened, and Fenrig's inert body was released onto the path.

"Is he dead?" Lizzie's voice quavered.

"Never mind him," said Rana coldly, kneeling by Petros. She cradled her brother's head in her lap, brushing the damp hair away from his face. Then, taking two small stones from her pocket, she placed them on her brother's forehead.

"*Vigilus!*"

Petros blinked, and fidgeted.

"Wha . . . what happened?"

"Armina won't mind. I borrowed some of her stones. Come here, Jack, and I'll fix your shoulder."

Jack tucked the sceptre and his sword into his waistband, and walked over to Petros and smiled down at him as Rana pressed a stone against his wound.

Owww!

There was a hiss and a brief puff of smoke, but then his shoulder felt fine. Reassured, Jack strode to the back of the cave and located the flag. Tentatively, he picked it up. About three feet by two, it weighed next to nothing.

Jack shivered, and the hairs on the back of his neck stood up. The flag glimmered in his hands.

"The *Mapa Mundi!*" he said in triumph. "It's ours!"

Jack edged back along the slippery path, cradling the flag in his hands. As he neared the mouth of the cave, the light showed the flag in more detail. It *was* an old map; the continents and seas were clearly visible in two big circles. It fluttered in his hands as a breeze came in from the sea.

"You missed all the action," he said to Petros with a broad grin.

"It looks like I missed it too."

"Grandpa!" Jack's joyous shout rang through the cave.

"The korrigan made the tunnel big enough! And once inside, my sceptre worked again, and I sped us along – like we were flying. Then I remembered something Konan had said. He 'stopped time flying' . . . Jack, show me the timer."

"How . . . how d'you know about that?"

"It's how Konan escaped: he must have slowed down time."

Jack fished the timer out of his pocket. There were still a few grains left in the top half.

"But we made it in time," he announced, puzzled. "We got past the Nucklat, and we've got the *Mapa Mundi*."

Petros had levered himself into a sitting position against the rock wall; a small trickle of blood oozed from the side of his head.

"Is it really the map?" he croaked.

"It is. And Jack was meant to get it," said his grandfather. "Now he has to turn it into the Sphere."

"Fenrig nearly got it," pointed out Rana. "He sneaked into the tunnel just after you. It's just as well we followed him. Grandpa's speed charm worked for him too."

Jack looked anxiously towards Fenrig's motionless body.

"I don't know why you're bothered about him," retorted Rana. "He was quite happy to see that monster kill you."

Jack saw that Fenrig was breathing, at least. Had he saved Fenrig, or was he just getting rid of the Nucklat?

"He couldn't just let Fenrig die, though," added Lizzie. "I know he's horrible, but getting squeezed to death . . . Ugh!"

"I couldn't let that happen." Jack spoke softly.

As he spoke, the flag in his hand began to curl up. The youngsters all looked on in amazement as, within a few seconds, it formed a perfect globe.

"It really is the Sphere!" gasped Petros, but he winced in pain as he spoke, and held his head.

Jack felt a flutter run through him, like . . . like the time he'd defeated Amadan the previous year. The third great Shian treasure! Now they could get the Kildashie out of Edinburgh.

But Grandpa was not sharing in Jack's elation.

"The sands are still running," he shouted, grasping the timer. "That means your task is not finished."

Grandpa Sandy tried to turn the timer on its side, but it would not go horizontal. Pausing for a moment, he directed his index finger at the timer and whispered, "*Planus!*"

The glass remained vertical.

"There's no time to lose. You must make the Sphere work."

Jack looked at the globe in his hands. What was it supposed to show? *Inside the Sphere I'll see my heart?*

He gazed hard at the globe. What was it showing him?

One of the circles faded; then the outline of Scotland and Ireland reappeared, filling the circle. Then, slowly, a single hexagonal column appeared in the sea off Mull.

"That's us! That must be this cave!"

Slowly, Ireland was replaced by a series of hexagonal columns. Then, beside them, a human figure slowly emerged. Below it the faintest of letters started to appear.

P . . . h . . . i . . .

Jack's heart nearly stopped.

. . . n . . . e . . . a . . . s . . .

25

The Giant's Bridge

Jack gulped.

"It's . . . it's my dad."

Rana peered inquisitively at the Sphere. She drew in her breath.

"He's . . . suspended, isn't he?"

Jack nodded. The pale figure hung there, apparently lifeless.

"So what are those shapes, then?" asked Lizzie, pointing to the strange columns next to Phineas' figure.

"They're columns, like these ones." Jack indicated the hexagonal pillars that extended from the cave wall to the sea outside. "I've never seen rocks like that before. It's like they're carved." He bent down so Petros could see.

Petros, still groggy, squinted at the Sphere.

"But they're in the wrong place. We're here," he indicated with his finger, "and they're over on Ireland."

Jack stared at the map.

How can we get over there? We've no boat . . . Aquines?

Jack concentrated hard, staring intently at the map. The columns seemed to float, rising and falling. What had Tamlina said, all those months ago? "*The cave o' the saint . . . The giant's bridge . . .*" Luka had called it St Fingal's tunnel . . . This must be St Fingal's cave . . . the cave of the saint.

So where's the giant's bridge?

Exasperated, Jack looked around.

"These columns are here . . . and the map says they're over in Ireland. And we need a giant's bridge to cross over." It would need to be a giant's bridge, right enough.

Something was missing.

My heart . . . "Inside the Sphere will see his heart." *What does that mean?*

Jack looked again at the Sphere.

"Jack, what do you really want?" His grandfather spoke softly.

A tear fell down Jack's cheek, but he didn't notice. He stared again at the map. The limp figure beside the columns now moved for the first time. It raised its head and its tiny eyes bored into Jack's. Jack saw its mouth open. A silent plea.

I want my dad.

"I wish . . . I wish the giant's bridge would appear."

And then his mind cleared. "*Columns awake,*" Tamlina had said. The columns on the Sphere were moving . . . they were awake.

"This must be the start of the bridge!" he shouted.

And another memory floated into his mind. That time he and Petros had gone to see Daid at Murkle's house, they'd had to sit through a torment of boredom. But what had Murkle said? Something about waking stone structures in giants' caves?

Jack aimed the sceptre at the columns opposite and shouted, "*Disuscito!*"

Nothing. The sea continued to draw in and out of the cave, a fine spray settling on the youngsters as they stood there.

Then, almost imperceptibly, the columns began to rise, just a little. But the ones outside the cave began to rise more, joining the others and forming a road over the sea. A bridge, in fact.

Or was it? The bridge only seemed to extend for twenty or thirty yards.

"You've done it, Jack!" shouted Grandpa. "Clever lad!"

A soft groaning sound greeted this announcement. Fenrig was starting to roll over onto his back, his every movement accompanied by a moan.

"He tried to steal the Sphere, Grandpa," asserted Lizzie. "And that monster nearly squeezed him to death." She pointed to the Nucklat's corpse. Gallons of slime had oozed out of its wounds, a sticky trail slowly dripping down into the sea.

"An impressive beast," replied Grandpa. "You have done exceedingly well to defeat it."

"The Sphere says your father's in Ireland. And the giant's bridge starts here," Rana stated. "But it only goes a few yards. Ireland's miles away."

Jack peered out to sea; then, with a shake of his head, said, "Then we'd better get started."

Petros tried to stand, but immediately stumbled.

"You're concussed," said Grandpa Sandy; "this next part is

too dangerous for you. Lizzie, can you take him back down the tunnel? Armina will see to him back on the island. Take Fenrig with you. Use this other sceptre." He whispered instructions in her ear.

"You mean I can't come across?" shouted Lizzie indignantly. "That's not fair!"

"Getting your brother back safely is important, and I'm entrusting Fenrig into your care too."

"I'd only hold them back." Petros squeezed his sister's arm.

Grandpa swiftly tied the young Brashat's arms behind him, and he was pushed unceremoniously over to the tunnel entrance. Petros walked slowly behind Fenrig, holding the rope, with Lizzie bringing up the rear. As they started off down the tunnel, Jack could hear Lizzie complaining to her brother.

"C'mon," said Jack. "Let's go."

Flicking the Sphere back into a flag, he tied it around his neck and strode out determinedly onto the column bridge, the sword still tucked into his waistband. As he marched forward, so his stomach lurched upwards – ten times stronger than when leaving the Shian square. The bridge extended swiftly in front of him. The columns seemed smaller – at most two feet across – and they bounced down and up slightly as he stepped on them.

Encouraged, Grandpa Sandy and Rana were quickly behind him, and within seconds the three were running over the curious bouncing bridge. The coastline to their left was several miles away, but as they advanced, so more of the bridge appeared in front of them. And, once they were well out to sea, the columns seemed to be getting thinner and the bridge narrower – not much wider than their feet.

"How long have we got?" asked Rana, anxiously balancing on the narrow bridge.

"Haven't you noticed?" laughed Jack as he looked back at his cousin. "We're giants!" The stretched feeling was . . . weird. Good . . . but weird.

Rana stopped for a moment, and looked around. The coast *was* nearer; and there was the occasional boat in the distance, but nothing close enough to guess size.

"Jack's right," replied Grandpa. "Only giants can use this bridge. We've grown."

Taking huge leaps over the springy columns, the three made quick progress down the coast. As the sun began to dip below the horizon, the Antrim shoreline came into view.

"Can't we rest for a bit?" puffed Rana, slowing down.

"Once we reach the shore," shouted Grandpa encouragingly.

As the coastline grew bigger, so the columnar shapes beneath them seemed to grow larger.

"We're shrinking!" shouted Jack. "That'll slow us down."

He pressed on, afraid that the sand timer would run through before they got to the shoreline . . . and, somewhere, his father. With relief, he saw the coast was just a hundred yards or so away now, but there was smoke there . . .

He slowed down.

What did the manuscripts say was at the end of the bridge? The pit of torment?

Jack had no time to think further: a flame shot past his head, out to sea. Then another. Soon, the three of them were being assailed by a volley of hurtling balls of fire. A great smoke obscured the end of the bridge.

And then Jack saw them, emerging slowly from the smoke. Five ... no, six fiery demons, all like the ones he'd seen ... where?

A sickly smell assailed him. What was it?

With a great shudder, he remembered. Phosphan. That meant ... Keldy. And Malevola.

Grandpa Sandy had been running just as fast as him. Now he saw his grandfather stumble and fall, twenty yards from the shore, as a fireball caught him on the leg. His sceptre fell, splashing into the water. He groaned loudly.

"Grandpa!" Jack shouted, running and kneeling over him.

The smoke cleared, revealing Malevola on the shoreline, the six demons huddled around her feet. Tall and majestic in the gloomy light, her eyes glared furiously at the three figures on the bridge. She held her sceptre in front of her, a glow emanating from it.

"Miserable creatures!" she thundered. "Did you think you could get past me?" And she brandished the ring on her left hand. Tamlina's ring. It flashed in the rays of the dying sun.

"Murderer!" shouted Jack, taking the sword from his belt.

Malevola cackled, an evil laugh that carried out over the water. "Pathetic Shian-lings. All you have done is bring the treasure to my hands."

Malevola held her right arm out towards Jack, and a beam shot out that quickly encased Jack's sword, melting it in seconds, leaving just a short stump. Dropping this, Jack instinctively tried to hide the flag behind him. Jack heard the sound of sobbing.

Grandpa was trying to talk, but the effort was too much. His shoulder and his leg reeked again, the same Phosphan stench that had lasted for weeks after Malevola's attack.

"We're Shian size again, aren't we?"

Jack nodded.

"Show me . . . the sand timer," he managed to whisper.

Jack searched in his pocket and drew out the timer.

"Planus!"

The timer still wouldn't turn on its side.

"A timer!" mocked Malevola. "By salt water? And they said you were clever, Sandy of the Stone. Yes, I know your name. I have made it my business to find out about you, and your houseful of brats."

Like Jack, Rana had cowered down by her grandfather. Now she stood up and faced Malevola.

"You're an evil witch! You don't deserve . . ."

But she got no further. A demon hurtled a ball of flame at her so quickly that she had no time to respond. Catching the side of her head, it set fire to her hair and knocked her off balance. She stumbled, then ran, screaming, into the sea.

Dumbstruck, Jack peered over the edge of the bridge, but there was no sign of his cousin. He stood up and made to run at the enchantress.

"No, Jack," his grandfather whispered. "That's what she wants."

Jack crouched down again, looking across at the shore, where Malevola was making for the bridge.

"She's limping!" he shouted.

"Yes, you foul child. Your hex at Keldy made its mark on

me. But if I cannot run to kill you as Malevola, then I will kill
you as . . ."

She held her arms above her head, then swept them both
down in an extravagant arc. There was a flash of smoke, and in
her place stood a wolfhound. Grey haired and five foot at the
shoulder, its mouth slavered and it snarled evilly.

Jack gulped. Uncle Doonya's Kynos hexes were not going
to be much use here.

The six demons, each no more than a foot high, cavorted
around the huge wolfhound as it started to slink slowly onto
the bridge. Never did its eyes leave Jack and his grandfather.
Its head slung low and its shoulders rippled as it slinked
towards its prey.

Jack looked around him. The bridge stretched back towards
St Fingal's cave, but there was no question of outrunning this
beast. And Grandpa's sceptre was lost, somewhere under the
waves, along with Rana.

As the wolfhound advanced, Jack heard his grandfather's
hoarse croak.

"Don't let the devils take me."

Grandpa? Scared? Then Jack saw the pain in his grandfather's
eyes. No, more than pain: agonised terror. The Phosphan was
bad enough, but to be tortured by demons . . .

The demons were advancing with the wolfhound as it
slinked forwards in the last light of the day. Fifteen yards away,
twelve . . . ten . . .

Demons. But Grandpa had called them devils.

The devil's shoestring!

Jack swiftly tied the flag around his neck and searched his
Sintura belt. Gratefully, he hooked his fingers around the tiny

wristlet. Slipping it onto his wrist, he pointed his arm at Malevola and shouted, "*Abcanidæ!*"

The wolfhound stumbled, its hind legs caught. Snarling furiously, it tried to jump forward, but its rear legs refused to work, and it slumped onto the bridge.

Great, thought Jack. *Now I'm supposed to use the jomo bag. But I've only got two kinds of dirt in there – from Dunvik and the island.*

The demons, uncertain for a moment at their leader's immobility, now began to advance on Jack and his grandfather again.

Six of them, thought Jack. *And I'm out ideas.*

His grandfather's sobs of pain were becoming weaker. Jack looked frantically around. He'd stopped Malevola – again – but still not finished her off. And her demons were about to make short work of him and Grandpa.

"Catch, Jack!"

With a great splash, Rana rose above the water's surface and threw the sceptre at him.

For half a second, Jack couldn't believe it. *She must've held her breath for a minute!* Then he turned the sceptre on the six small demons and uttered, "*Gosol!*"

A bolt shot from the sceptre. The six demons screamed and began to swirl rapidly around. In seconds they were small balls of flame, spinning round so quickly they formed a ring of fire. Then, with a loud scream, the flames rose into the air and arced up and then down, hitting the water beside the bridge with a great hiss of steam. The water bubbled for a moment, then settled.

Jack now aimed the sceptre at the wolfhound as it lay

snarling. It tried to get up, and managed to half-rise before collapsing on the bridge again.

"No, Jack," Grandpa Sandy gasped.

"Spare her?" Rana demanded incredulously as she scrambled onto the bridge. "Finish her off, Jack."

"The ring. Get the ring back first."

Rana stooped down and picked up the stump of Jack's sword. She was swiftly on the wolfhound, which snapped and tried to bite her, but it was weak, and she deftly sliced off the paw on which Tamlina's Triple-S ring sat. Slipping the ring off the bloody paw, she held it up triumphantly and asked, "Can I do it? Please? I saw a really good hex in one of Armina's books."

Smiling, Jack shrugged and handed her the sceptre. Carefully, Rana put the ring on the chain around her neck and pointed the sceptre at the whimpering beast. It looked up at her in mute appeal and wagged its tail.

Rana hesitated.

But just for a moment. A renewed gasp of pain from her grandfather removed all doubt from her mind.

"*Til Helvete!*"

The sceptre sparkled; a beam shot from it and hit the wolfhound as it lay on the bridge. With a great flash, the beast disappeared.

Silence.

"A Norse hex?" croaked Grandpa in wonder.

"It had to be: she was from Tula. Only a Norse hex would work."

A distant howl began, and the sea, which had been calm, suddenly started to froth and foam. Waves hit the bridge and sprayed up, soaking Jack, Rana and Grandpa. A thunderclap rent the air and great lumps of rain began to fall.

The hexagonal columns started to sink down.

"The bridge is going!" Jack shouted.

He stooped down, picked up the swordfish stump and managed to lever his grandfather up to a sitting position.

"You've got to walk, Grandpa. It's only twenty yards."

But Grandpa Sandy was too weak for even this. Before he had managed to stand, the bridge was below the water. He stumbled forward, splashing as the waves rose up.

"Make sure the sceptre's safe!" Jack shouted at Rana. And he pushed his grandfather off the bridge.

26
The Pit of Torment

Grandpa Sandy gasped in surprise, then sank beneath the waves.

He surfaced; an outraged splutter was mixed with an urgent intake of air, then he went under again.

Jack jumped in. Cupping the old man's chin firmly in his left hand, he swam furiously for the shore. His grandfather's struggles made the task no easier, but he thankfully had only a short distance to swim.

Rana had waded to the shore on the remnants of the disappearing bridge, but as she made the shoreline the last of the sea columns vanished. She helped an exhausted Jack to drag their grandfather clear of the water, and as they got further above the shoreline the sea became calm again. The wind blew the last of the clouds away as the moon rose in the darkening sky.

Jack huffed as he took deep breaths in.

"I'm sorry, Grandpa. But you were going to take ages, and the bridge was sinking."

His grandfather's feeble wave seemed to indicate that he understood.

"I've got the sceptre," said Rana helpfully.

"Then let's get a fire going. Is there any shelter?"

Rana scanned the rocky shore.

"There's a rock overhang up there."

Dragged upright by Jack, Grandpa Sandy leant on his shoulder as he hobbled up the beach.

At least last time I had Ossian to help me. Grandpa weighs a ton.

Rana, having scampered ahead, now came back and joined Jack in helping their grandfather to where a jutting rock provided some shelter.

"I must rest," he gasped, collapsing down onto coarse, dirty sand.

"The last time we did this, a lion jumped out at us," remarked Jack, as he stuffed a little of the dirt into his jomo bag.

"Well, Marco's not here. Go and get some firewood. Then I can look at Grandpa's wounds," said Rana.

Jack soon returned with some driftwood and used the sceptre to light a fire.

"*Ignitas!*" Seeing Rana's look of surprise, he added, "Ossian showed me."

The fire smouldered in the stiff breeze, producing more smoke than light.

"Is that the best you could do?" demanded Rana.

"Well, why don't *you* go and look for some dry wood? I'm cold."

"We're *all* cold," Rana shouted back.

"Please." Their grandfather's hoarse whisper reached them. "Don't argue. We must conserve our strength."

"What happened to your leg, Grandpa?" asked Rana anxiously.

"It was Malevola, wasn't it?" said Jack. "She opened the Phosphan wounds again."

Grandpa Sandy nodded, wincing with pain. The Phosphan stench was unmistakable.

"What do we do now?" Rana grimaced as the fumes assailed her nostrils.

"We must find Phineas," whispered Grandpa. "Jack, show me the timer."

In the feeble light of the fire, Jack held it for his grandfather to see. There were only a few grains of sand left in the top chamber, and it still wouldn't tip onto its side.

"We must get away from the sea. Then we've a chance with the timer."

With infinite difficulty, Grandpa Sandy forced himself to stand, leaning on Jack once more. He looked out towards the sea again.

"Where did the bridge end?"

"Just over there," answered Rana. "Pretty much towards us if it hadn't sunk."

"Then the cave it is." Grandpa Sandy held the sceptre aloft, its ruby glowing in the dark, and began to hobble towards the rear of the cave.

"Wait a minute. Grandpa," said Jack, almost buckling under

the weight. "What's supposed to be at the bridge end? Cosmo said something about the pit of . . ."

He got no further. The floor of the cave opened, and all three tumbled into a slimy whirlpool. Nearly suffocating with the wet mud, they were all swirled around, faster and faster, and sucked deeper into the centre of the vortex.

"Keep hold of the Sph . . . !" gasped Grandpa, just before being sucked down below the surface.

Jack took a deep breath just as he too disappeared into the slime.

Jack knew he was falling, but it didn't feel like regular falling. Sort of . . . slower; he had time to look around him. There was Grandpa, also falling, just a bit below him. And Rana was above him, still swirling round as she fell through the . . . what? What was this?

There was a jolt, and a crack. Jack suddenly felt very cold, and a wailing noise, which had started softly, now deafened him.

With a thump he came to land, partially over his grandfather's leg.

"Ayabass . . . !" His grandfather stifled an oath as a wave of terrifying pain shot through him.

Jack rolled to the side to release his grandfather's leg, but realised that he was on a narrow shelf of rock. A rock wall behind; in front, a long drop.

"Help! Jack!" screamed Rana as she half-landed on Jack and slipped off the rock shelf.

Jack thrust his right hand out and caught Rana's arm . . . But her arm was all slimy, and his grip was slipping . . . He had her around the wrist now . . .

If I'd time, I could get myself free to lift her back up.

A flash of realisation. Jack whipped the sand timer out of his pocket and whispered, "*Planus!*"

The last dozen grains of sand in the upper chamber now halted.

Everything halted.

He had Rana by the wrist, but she wasn't slipping any more. There was an eerie stillness all around him. Breathing heavily, he looked at the timer, now on its side.

Jack leant over and grabbed the bottom edge of his grandfather's cloak, then reached down with his left hand and used it to wipe Rana's arm dry. Then he reached down with both hands and hauled her up onto the rock shelf.

Rana made no sound as she lay there. His grandfather's moans had stopped too. Jack looked again at the horizontal sand timer. The emeralds at either end glowed brightly, lighting up the rock shelf on which he was perched. Jack stared at it.

Have I stopped time?

Even as he watched, the upper chamber rose slightly, and with a loud *clunk!* a grain of sand slipped through the opening. Eleven grains left.

Jack peered over the edge of the shelf. There was nothing to see, really, just a long, dark drop. Finding a small pebble, he threw it down.

No sound from that.

Great. What now?

Use the Sphere. Jack untied the *Mapa Mundi* flag from around his neck and held it out in front of him. As he did so, it formed into the Sphere again. He looked inside, expecting to see his father. But it was Rana's face that he saw staring back at him. She had something shiny around her neck.

Looking over to where Rana lay motionless, Jack saw Tamlina's ring on his cousin's neck chain. Slipping the chain off, he put it over his own head. It nestled in comfortably behind his shirt. He turned back to the Sphere.

Blank. Nothing.

Perplexed, Jack looked around him. What had Cosmo said? *The pit of torment.* This was a pit, all right. But torment?

And then the wailing began again, from far below. Wails, worse than the worst journey along the low road. An icy blast ran through Jack.

Whose torment? Who's here?

Ghostly wisps began to rise out of the pit now: tortured faces, whirling around his head, screaming in agony. And a coldness, too. The sea had been cold, and the wind on the beach. Then the whirlpool slime: that had been freezing. But this was something far worse: like a winter blast that drives ice right into your heart and brain.

And Jack remembered Trog's misery, the torment he said he'd suffered each day. The torment he thought would only be relieved when he got hold of the *Mapa Mundi*. But Jack had had the vision; he'd been meant to find the Sphere. Jack tried to shrug the nausea off and looked at the Sphere again. Why wouldn't it show him anything?

The upper chamber of the sand timer rose again, and with another *clunk!* another grain of sand slipped through. Ten grains.

Well, I'm obviously not meant to stop here. And I can't carry the others.

Pocketing the timer and grabbing his grandfather's sceptre, Jack stood up. Which way? The rock shelf stretched to right and left, but Jack couldn't see anything in particular either way. He stared again at the Sphere.

Please. Please let me see which way to go. I have to find my father.

Slowly, agonisingly slowly, the limp figure of Phineas reappeared in the Sphere. His head hung down again, but next to him was a tall figure in a grey cloak. Her pale face was emotionless, her eyes staring directly forward. Then she raised her right arm and slowly beckoned with her index finger. Her eyes sparkled.

Which way?

"To your left."

It was like a whisper in his ear, but Jack heard it clearly. He looked around, though he knew there was no one there. No one but the ghostly faces.

My left. Right.

Jack flipped the Sphere back to a flag and tied it around his neck once more. Then he started to edge along the rock shelf, but it was no more than a foot wide. Even at Shian size, there was precious little room for error. His grandfather's sceptre gave off a dim light, but no more.

Don't look down.

Jack felt a clunk from his pocket and knew that another grain in the timer had fallen. Nine left.

Quick, quick, quick. Got to get there.

But where? The inside of the pit had not changed in any way as Jack edged along the rock shelf. Where was he going? Water running down the rock walls made the shelf slippery. And then Jack began to slide. He tried to keep his feet close to the wall, but then his sceptre struck a jutting-out rock. He sprawled helplessly over the edge.

Oh no.

And yet as Jack fell, once again it was in slow motion. He saw a rope bridge, V-shaped with two handrails and a central wooden path, strung across the pit. As he approached, Jack grabbed it and clung on for dear life. Slowly the bridge stopped swinging and Jack looked down. Still no bottom in sight, and neither end was in view.

"This way."

The same whisper in his ear directed him to his left, and he set off along the bridge. It swung with his walking movements, a giddy, unpleasant feeling that made him think about the long drop below. This would be easier using both rails. Jack tucked the sceptre into his waistband once more and started walking.

Without the glow from his sceptre, Jack was walking blind, but he kept going. *Clunk!* Another grain of sand fell. Eight left. Jack quickened his pace.

It's all for nothing if I don't get there soon – wherever "there" is.

Jack had been scurrying along the rope bridge for what seemed like hours. The thoughts inside his head whirled around: *I'll never get there. I'll be walking this bridge forever, and my father will die.*

He shook his head, trying to clear the bad thoughts.

Got to keep going. Rescue Dad, then go back for Rana and Grandpa. Got to keep going. Gosol will help.

After an eternity – *Clunk!* Only seven grains left now – Jack saw a light ahead. Increasing pace, he started to jog, then felt the sceptre work loose from his belt.

No, need to have that. Don't know what I'll meet at the end.

He took the sceptre from his waistband and advanced cautiously. The rope bridge gradually sloped upwards. *I must be near the end.*

And he was. Jack could see a rock wall looming in front of him and a small platform where the rope bridge ended.

Seven grains. At this rate I've got some time left.

Climbing gratefully onto the platform, he saw a doorway cut into the rock face. Passing through, he came upon a cavernous dimly lit chamber. The walls were in shadow, but in the centre sat an old woman wearing a grey cloak.

His footsteps echoed around the chamber. She didn't look up.

"So, ye've come for Phineas o' Rangie, have ye?"

The doorway behind him sealed itself over.

27
The Grey

Jack looked at the old woman, who sat surrounded by flickering candles within a small clearing. Her hood almost covered her head. Had she spoken? The voice had had a strange quality about it that he couldn't define. Slow and husky, but not just dry: *aged*, somehow.

"My . . . my father . . ." Jack managed to stutter.

"And ye hae used that accursed timepiece tae cheat yer way in here."

Jack took the sand timer from his pocket. With a sense of relief he saw that it remained almost horizontal – there were still seven grains left. Jack edged cautiously forward; still the old woman didn't move. Jack looked around anxiously. Where was his father?

"Ye bettered Konan, eh? That scheming Brashat would never surrender his meddlesome sand piece." Her sluggish voice was no less harsh. "But to bring it here was foolish. Meet my Taniwah."

A splash from behind her confirmed to Jack that the cave was far from dry, but wetness was not his main concern. Even in the dim light Jack could see the Taniwah lizard rising slowly at the back of the cave, its single eye glinting in the gloom.

Taniwahs! Quick! What's Finbogie taught me about them?

With a rising panic, Jack could think of nothing about these creatures, except that you must avoid their gaze — that was instant death. Jack grasped the stump of his sword — well, it had helped him against the Nucklat. But a short stump would be no use against this monster. And the creature was emerging from the pool in which it had been resting. Jack backed away, but found the entrance way gone. He squinted at the beast.

I've heard something else. Who else was talking about them? If only I could see better. It's a full moon outside.

The moon!

Taniwahs hate moonlight. Murkle had shouted that at Cosmo. *But we're deep underground.*

"Up, Balor, my friend." The Grey's husky voice called out triumphantly.

I've heard it somewhere . . . Of course! Armina!

Jack had no time to act. The Taniwah now rose several feet above the surface, water splashing towards Jack. Caught unawares, he dropped the sand timer. As it fell to the ground, a tiny splash of seawater caught it and it uprighted itself.

No!

Jack tried to turn it horizontal again, but some unstoppable force was pushing it up. The last few grains quickly dropped into the lower chamber. And Jack saw to his horror that the old grey woman was starting to rise.

"Now devour him, my Balor." Her voice was no longer slow and was even more menacing.

With a roar that echoed around the cave, the Taniwah lunged at Jack. His heart in his mouth, Jack thrust his grandfather's sceptre towards the great lizard.

"*Lunalumen!*"

It wasn't like a human light switch being flicked — Jack had seen that — but the cave filled rapidly with a moonlit glow. The Taniwah dropped, motionless, just a foot short of Jack. Its mouth agape, Jack could see dozens of sharp, pointed teeth.

That was close.

With a shriek, the Grey shielded her eyes from the unaccustomed light. Jack gripped the swordfish stump and drove the full six inches into the top of the Taniwah's head. There was a spurt of blood, then a steady trickle. And then Jack saw him. Suspended behind the Grey, near the cave wall's hexagonal columns, was his father. His limp body hung with no visible means of support. Tattered rags did little to hide his emaciated condition.

"The sand has run out, ye meddling boy." The Grey, still shielding her eyes, cackled triumphantly. "See, he breathes his last."

A muted gasp emerged from Phineas' gaunt frame.

No. Please no. I can't have come all this way for him to die on me.

Jack sank to the ground, a great wave of despair rising from his core. Tears welled up, and without thinking Jack wiped his eyes with the flag still tied around his neck.

The Sphere!

The Grey was still shielding her eyes. Hurriedly, Jack untied the flag, and it formed into the Sphere once more. Jack gazed at it. In one circle the sand timer appeared, then inverted itself.

I've got to turn it over!

Hurriedly, Jack turned the timer over and saw with relief that the grains were running through.

I guess that buys me some time . . .

Jack saw a shape emerging in the other circle . . . the Chalice. It was as Jack remembered it from Dunvik the previous year. Comgall the monk had given him the Chalice, and it had revived his grandfather.

It can do the same for my dad! But . . . it's in the Stone Room in Edinburgh.

Then the Chalice image turned into the fiery outline he'd seen in Claville and Edinburgh.

The memory of the Chalice is enough?!

And quietly, a word came to Jack, a word Marco and Trog had used repeatedly on the island: "I believe . . ."

"Only believe . . ."

I believe the Chalice can bring my father back.

How had Cosmo explained the conjuring of the fiery chalice? It hit Jack in a flash, and he grasped the still glowing sceptre.

"Calixignis!"

Sketching in the air before him, Jack's heart raced as he saw the fiery outline of the Chalice appear, triple-S spirals and all. The flames crackled in the damp air.

Alerted by the sound, the Grey risked a peek at Jack as he tied the flag around his neck once more. Squinting in the unaccustomed brightness, she caught sight of the fiery outline. Despite the pain this obviously caused her, Jack saw her eyes open wide.

"The Cha . . ." she gurgled.

I've got her, thought Jack. *She can't fight the power of the Chalice.*

And it seemed as if he was right. His father, still suspended, gasped audibly.

He's not dead! The sand timer worked!

Jack willed the Chalice to float over to where his father hung, some fifteen yards away. The fiery outline hovered in front of Phineas.

"You dare to defy my power?" shrieked the Grey. "I will not be beaten by a mere Shian boy."

"But you can see: he's not dead," taunted Jack.

"You have crossed into my domain," she cackled, and Jack saw to his horror that she was now able to look straight at him without squinting.

Panic-stricken, he grasped the sceptre and thrust the glowing end towards her.

"*Lunalumen!*"

"Your charms will not work for long here, wretch. Every minute you spend here brings you closer to my power. *Cadaveros!*"

With that, she waved her left arm in an arc and the temperature plummeted. Jack had no time to react, for he was encased once again by the streaming ghostly faces that had swept around him in the pit. Tortured faces, their agonised features screaming icily at him. And he remembered Trog again, his sorrow and hopelessness. The fiery Chalice disappeared in a puff of smoke. Once more Jack sank to his knees, the despair in him almost complete.

And then the ghosts were gone again, and the icy blasts had stopped. Jack looked up. The Grey was standing over him now, smiling evilly.

"Puny little Shian," she mocked. "Daring to take what's mine. But you have spirit. Let us see how much you value your father's precious life."

She clicked her fingers, and by the cave wall below Phineas, on a large hexagonal shelf of rock, appeared Rana and Grandpa Sandy. Rana sat hunched, silent, her hands out towards Jack, imploringly. Tears streamed down her face. Grandpa lay sprawled awkwardly.

"While the timepiece sits right, they are awake." The Grey indicated the timer, and Jack could see the top half was full, the grains running steadily through.

The Phosphan smell reached Jack and he felt a familiar sensation of nausea. His grandfather was definitely there. But neither his grandfather nor Rana made any sound.

"Well then, my Shian halfling, let us see how much you truly wish your father's return. His life for theirs. Deal?"

Jack's heart skipped several beats.

A deal? You can't trade lives like they're old toys.

"So which do you love more?" the old woman crowed. She pointed her right index finger at Phineas, and his body slumped down next to Rana.

Jack longed to turn the flag into the Sphere once more, but did not dare risk this with the Grey looking on.

I need help. Where's my true path now?

Jack felt his mind whirl for a while, and then suddenly clear.

"The Grey doesn't do deals."

The words echoed in Jack's head. Who had spoken? Not Grandpa, nor Rana. Could it have been his father? Jack looked over to his father's body, but it appeared lifeless.

Hang on – we talked about this last year. Konan escaped; he didn't make a deal.

"Take your time, boy. That's one thing I'll never run out of." The Grey cackled as she settled back on her stool, regarding Jack with malevolent relish.

Time . . . What is it about time?

The sand timer . . . Konan had got away because he'd slowed time down; he'd caught the Grey unawares. Jack looked over to where the Grey sat.

I know she's trying to trick me, but as long as she thinks I'm deciding who to take with me, she won't do anything.

"Meddlesome child!" the Grey muttered, as she sat hunched in her chair. "*Emeta!*" Casually, she waved her right arm at Jack, and a fresh wave of nausea and despair engulfed him.

Unable to stop himself, Jack vomited.

This place is desperate. I've got to get out of here.

Jack tried to think of the warm, bright days of the last month . . . roaming the island . . . going fishing with Rana . . . *Anything to make me feel happier.*

It didn't really work, though, and he heaved again as the sickness clutched at his stomach.

The Grey, satisfied that her hex was keeping Jack occupied, had settled quietly – she even seemed to be dozing. Her eyes were shut, anyway.

Jack noted that his grandfather's sceptre was glowing brightly; the cave still looked as if moonlight was getting in.

But the Lunalumen charm hadn't worked on the Grey for long.

Checking that the Grey was still dozing, Jack untied the flag and it formed into the Sphere again. The blank circles were clear, and then slowly, ever so slowly, two images appeared: the sand timer and the sun. The sun's image glowed brightly.

Now daylight: that would really dazzle her. But we're deep underground. At least I think we are; I seemed to fall for ages. And it's night-time now, hours before daylight – if I can let it in. Will she wait that long?

Jack looked around the cave. There was fresh air coming from somewhere, but no light. *It's night-time.*

Night-time. Time.

The word kept playing in Jack's mind. He looked at the Sphere once more. The sun image glowed brighter than ever.

Dawn's hours away.

Jack forced himself to concentrate.

It's like I would have to make it the quickest night ever . . . Like at Oestre.

Jack nearly jumped at the thought. Grandpa said they'd speeded time up that night.

Speeding time up may make my dad's time run out . . . but how long has he got . . . ?

Jack felt sick again and clamped his mouth tight shut. He looked surreptitiously over to the sand timer. The grains were passing through.

She doesn't want me to stop time again. But I won't: I'll speed it up!

As cautiously as he could, Jack tied the flag around his neck and lowered the sceptre so that it pointed at the sand timer.

"*Fugitemp!*"

The Grey, huddled on her stool, did not appear to notice as a ray shot from the sceptre. The sand timer rose briefly, and as it settled again Jack saw to his delight that the grains were running through much more quickly.

Uuurgh!

His delight was tempered immediately as the despair and nausea swept over him again – only much worse. He retched.

I can't take much more of this . . .

Jack gulped back another dry heave and tried to dispel the feeling of wretchedness in his gut.

OK. So the night's passing faster. But I've still got to get my family out of here.

The Grey's Emeta curse was still working – Jack had never felt so awful in his life. Even Trog's misery was better than this. But Jack forced himself to remain alert.

She thinks she's got time on her side; I've got to beat her at her own game.

Gradually, Jack's hopes began to rise. The Grey remained huddled on her stool, apparently asleep . . . and the sand continued to rush through the timer. The bottom chamber was more than half full now . . .

As long as my dad is still alive . . .

Jack tried to imagine what he would do when he felt dawn had arrived . . . Three quarters . . .

Fresh air was coming from somewhere, and Marco's words came back to him: "Gosol will let in the light, even through the tiniest crack."

Just a glimpse of daylight would be enough. *Light – that will do for the Grey.*

The sands were slipping through so easily ... *Can't be long now.* Jack looked over to his family. Only Rana looked awake, and she obviously couldn't speak; Phineas and Grandpa remained slumped.

The Grey coughed and came to. Looking around curiously, her gaze came to rest on Jack.

"I see ye've still no' made up yer mind, boy," she snarled. "Well, it matters little. None o' ye shall leave here."

She paused.

"Ye're up to some Shian trickery ... I can feel it. Whit have ye done?" Her steely eyes bored into Jack. Then she looked down to the sand timer, and with a shriek she leapt at Jack.

"Filthy Shianling!"

Jack gabbed the sceptre and thrust it towards her.

"*Lunalumen!*"

With a contemptuous swipe, the Grey sent the sceptre, still glowing, spinning to the side of the cave. Gripping Jack by the neck, she held him at arm's length, his legs dangling. Through the flag tied round his neck, Jack felt her fingers clutching his throat. He fought desperately for breath, kicking and squirming, but the Grey just stared at him scornfully. As Jack started to black out, she threw him dismissively over towards the others.

"Now I will put an end to you all, Shian wretches!"

Fighting for breath, Jack instinctively put his hands up to his neck – and through his shirt front he felt Tamlina's ring on Rana's chain. Hurriedly, he pulled out the ring and put it on his middle finger. Struggling to his feet, he held his hand up to the Grey.

She stopped in her tracks.

"No ... no ..." She backed away, her eyes wide open in horror.

Keeping his eye on her, Jack stooped down and retrieved the sceptre.

And then the Grey stopped retreating and faced Jack, malice returning to her eyes.

"Ye have ta'en the sacred ring from my sister Malevola. Ye'll pay for that." And she advanced cautiously.

Jack gulped. He'd banked on Tamlina's ring having more effect than that.

The Grey edged towards Jack, her right arm outstretched.

"Give me the ring, boy."

Jack looked around in desperation. So much for the escape plan.

And then the sweetest sound ever to reach his ears echoed around the cave. Birdsong.

Looking for the source of the sound, Jack saw a small crack of light directly above him. As the Grey neared, he held the sceptre aloft and called out, "*Gosol!*"

The beam from the sceptre shot upwards, hitting the cave ceiling. Instantly, a flood of bright light filled the cave. The Grey staggered back, screeching hideously, sweeping her cloak around her face. Shrieking, she fled to the far depths of the cave, her curses getting fainter as she ran.

Retreating back to the hexagonal shelf on which his family lay slumped, Jack struck the rock floor firmly with the sceptre and shouted, "*Disuscito!*"

This time there was no delay. The column woke instantly and began to rise, and as it did so, Grandpa Sandy and Phineas stirred. In seconds, the four had reached the cave ceiling and were passing through the hole Jack had blasted. In half a minute, they were staring at the beach as it glowed in the early morning light.

But Jack knew they had no time to rest.

"Come on!" He pulled his father off the column and urged Rana to do the same with Grandpa. "We must get away."

"But where can we go?" asked Rana plaintively as Grandpa and Phineas got unsteadily to their feet.

A rumbling sound came from below. Jack looked round as a flame erupted from the hole in the ground through which they had just emerged.

"Anywhere." Jack began half-dragging his father along the beach.

28

We Are Sailing

The flames started in earnest now. Jack felt a wave of heat as he struggled to pull his father along the beach and away from the Grey's cave. Phineas stumbled forward, only just able to stand. Panic-stricken, Jack realised that he had no hope of getting far: though emaciated, his father's body was still too heavy for him. Rana was faring no better with Grandpa: though he could stand – just – he was not up to fleeing.

Jack looked round and saw three wic-elves emerge from the hole leading down into the cave. Only slightly smaller than Jack, their eyes blazed, and they brandished their talon-like claws menacingly.

"Jack! Help!" Rana screamed as Grandpa Sandy fell.

Jack allowed his father to crumple onto the beach and ran over to his grandfather.

"Grandpa! You've got to get up! The wic-elves are coming."

The three creatures, only yards away, fizzled with heat. One hurled a fireball, which sizzled Rana's hair as it flew past. Another caught Jack on the foot, and he yelped with pain. The smell of Grandpa's Phosphan burns assailed Jack once more.

"Feel in my pouch," whispered Grandpa, frantically fumbling with the folds of his cloak.

Determinedly ignoring the searing pain in his foot, Jack put his hand inside the pouch and felt a tiny stone. Withdrawing it, he saw that it was bright green, with a tiny flaw inside. A tiny ship-shaped flaw.

"*Nautilus!*"

Grandpa Sandy's whisper was barely audible, but with a sudden *whoosh!* a great wind blew in from behind them. The wic-elves halted . . . Jack heard the sound of running feet on the pebbly beach behind him . . . And suddenly half a dozen cloaked figures had run past Jack and the others, their sceptres drawn.

"*Exflagro!*"

The wic-elves seemed to evaporate as a series of bolts flew from the sceptres.

"Come on," said one of the men. "Their brothers won't be far behind."

Jack and the others were lifted up unceremoniously, and the figures made swiftly for the sea. Splashing into the shallows, the rescuers manhandled the four into a waiting boat. Grandpa Sandy gasped in pain as he was bundled on board; Phineas, limp as a rag doll, made no sound.

"Push out!" called one of the figures, and two of the others put their shoulders to the bow and heaved the craft into deeper water. Another two quickly hoisted the mainsail, and within a minute they were sailing away from the beach. Jack, amazed at the skill with which these men had launched the boat, could only look on in wonder.

"Who . . . who are you?" he managed to utter.

"Don't say ye don't remember me, Jack." One of the figures laughed. "Ah, we came all the way to Rangie to see ye at Oestre; had ye forgotten? I'm Enda; that's Dermot."

"You're McCools!" cried Rana, looking from one to the other. A great wave of relief flooded through her, and she burst into tears.

"Ah, we're not as bad as all that," said Dermot. "Just as well your grandfather kept that charm stone I gave him, though. Those wic-elves aren't out to play, but they won't come far out to sea. We'll be all right now."

Struggling to keep the tears out of his eyes, Jack looked pleadingly at Enda.

"Can you help my dad?"

The tall figure looked down as Jack cradled his father's head in his lap.

"We're sailors, not physicians."

"Luka's a physician," shouted Rana. "Head for the island; we can call him back."

"Would that be Ilanbeg?" Enda enquired.

Rana and Jack both nodded assent.

"We'll be there in no time. Sure, it's not far."

The McCool's sense of time, however, was not the same as Jack's or Rana's. With a fair wind behind them, the small boat was making progress and the Antrim coast behind them retreated, but it was soon clear that the journey would take more than a day, even with summer charms. Placing Phineas and Grandpa in the prow of the boat to rest, Jack and Rana recounted all they could remember of their journey over from St Fingal's cave and down into the Grey's pit.

"So ye used the giant's bridge?" asked Dermot. "Ye're blessed, then. It's centuries since that was used."

"It was the Sphere that raised it," added Rana. "Show him, Jack."

Jack fingered the flag around his neck, uncertain whether to show this to the McCools. *But they must be on our side*, he thought, and untied the flag. As it formed into the Sphere, he felt a wave of interest sweep the boat.

"Is that really the *Mapa Mundi*?" enquired Telos, who had been in the prow with Grandpa and Phineas. "Fair play to ye."

He moved towards Jack, who shrank back. Telos stood over him, and Jack saw a mixture of emotions in the man's eyes: desire and hunger — and fear. As Telos extended his hand, Jack squirmed backwards.

"Leave him be, man," ordered Enda. "We'll decide what happens when we get to Ilanbeg."

Rana, oblivious to the short drama that had just played out, continued, "And he used it in the Grey's cave."

"Ye got away from the Grey?" Enda was clearly impressed.

"I doubt she's beat," added Dermot. "I'm not sure any of us will live long enough to see that happen. But getting away from her — that's a victory."

"And rescuing his dad," chimed in Rana.

They looked over at Phineas' wasted body. Nobody spoke.

It was late the following afternoon before Jack felt sure that he could recognise landmarks in the coast off to their right.

"I remember that headland," he shouted, pointing to a rocky outcrop. "It was smaller when we were on the bridge, though." He flicked the Sphere, transforming it back into a flag, which he tied around his neck.

"Ilanbeg's not far," said Enda. "We'd better let your family know that we're coming."

He looked up at the sky for a moment, then put two fingers to his mouth and blew a sharp whistle. A seagull whirled round before coming to rest on the side of the boat. Offering it some scraps of food, Enda uttered a series of guttural sounds that neither Jack nor Rana understood. The bird flew off, squawking harshly.

After a while Enda started to haul down the sail, and the boat began to drift in towards a bay.

"Is this Ilanbeg?" enquired Rana. "We left by the tunnel."

"Can't you see?" laughed Dermot. "There's Luka. I'd recognise him anywhere."

Jack and Rana scanned the bay and the fields beyond it, but could see nothing more than a calf at the water's edge.

"There's no one there," stated Jack.

The boat drifted into the shallows and beached itself on gravelly sand.

"We'll give ye a hand out," announced Enda.

He lifted first Rana, then Jack over the side of the boat into the arms of one of his comrades, who waded the short distance ashore. As Dermot deposited him on the beach, Jack – human size once more – saw Luka stride forwards. Jack rubbed his eyes in astonishment.

"I understand you've got some casualties." The old man smiled at him.

"Where . . . where did you come from?"

"Let's get you all out of the boat."

Enda and the others between them were carrying Phineas and Grandpa Sandy over the side of the boat and ashore. Lying the two men down on the beach, they ushered Luka forward. Luka made a cursory inspection, then asked them to carry the two invalids up to the house.

"Where did the calf go?" Rana was standing beside her cousin. "I'm sure Luka wasn't on the beach before."

Jack was staring at the place where the calf had been. There was a funny pattern there – like a circle. A dozen small stones in the sand. He felt in his pocket. The yucca fibres were oozing oil.

"He's a sh—"

"Come on now," Enda called over.

The litter party had reached the top of the bay, and was disappearing out of sight. The McCools were marching almost as fast as the two youngsters could run, and Jack and Rana took some time to catch up. Nearing the house (still a ruin from the outside), the youngsters ran ahead and were met by Aunt Katie and Aunt Dorcas, closely followed by Petros.

Aunt Katie clutched Rana to her chest, unable to speak. Petros stopped as he reached Jack, smiling sheepishly.

"You got on all right, then."

Jack didn't speak, but indicated the McCool party that was approaching quickly. As they arrived, Luka and Armina took Phineas and Grandpa Sandy indoors, ushering the others outside.

Marco led Uncle Hart, his eyes still bandaged, up to Jack.

"You've done well, lad. You've brought my brother back."
Uncle Hart's voice croaked with emotion.

Jack didn't know what to say. He'd dreamt about this day
for such a long time, but his father was so nearly dead he still
didn't dare hope that all would be well.

"And you've brought back the *Mapa Mundi*," said Marco.
"May I see it?"

Jack untied the flag from around his neck and presented it
to Marco. It remained as a flag, the two circles showing their
maps.

"It's only the Sphere for Shian," explained Jack.

Marco smiled. "I know, but it's beautiful for us too. It holds
many secrets. You keep it for now. We'll need to attend to our
new guests."

"Where are all the others?" enquired Rana.

"Finbogie took them down to Trog's bay," explained Petros.
"Trog wanted to ask Fenrig's forgiveness for something. They
should be back soon."

"I want Trog to hold the flag," stated Jack. "He deserves to."

Marco smiled at him. "I'm sure he'd like that."

"Will . . . will my father be all right?" stammered Jack.

Marco looked towards the house and indicated to Jack that
Luka was beckoning them in. Nervously, Jack stumbled over
to the odd-looking house. With relief, he saw that Luka was
smiling.

"Jack," mumbled Grandpa Sandy as Jack entered. "You've
done it again. And you've brought our Phineas back to us."

"Is he . . . going to be all right?"

"He's weak," replied Luka, as he ushered Jack upstairs to
where Phineas was stretched out on one of the beds. "More

than ten years suspended is brutal. And by the looks of it you brought him back just in time. But I can get him better – in time."

"The Grey said he'd breathed his last, but I thought of the Chalice, and that seemed to bring him back."

"You did well, then. And when the time is right, he'll tell you the secret that the Grey never got from him – about the Stone key."

"But that's just a myth!" exclaimed Jack.

"On the contrary," continued Luka. "Your father is one of very few who knew something particular about the Stone in Edinburgh. Tamlina was another, though she didn't know that he knew. A shame, that: if she had, she might have saved him from being taken by the Grey."

"But you defeated the Grey," added Marco. "And to bring the *Mapa Mundi* back, that was bold. You showed your bravery and courage – well done."

Jack blushed and glanced through the small window. To his delight he saw Finbogie leading Trog and the others up to the house. He looked over to where his father lay. Despite what Luka had said, it was hard to believe he was really alive. But he trusted the physician.

"Can I show Trog the flag?" he enquired.

"Of course." Luka nodded at the door, and Jack gratefully bounded down the stairs.

He met Trog just in front of the house. The Norseman stopped, a look of uncertainty on his face. Jack untied the flag from around his neck and presented it to the warrior-savant. Trog, initially hesitant, reached forward and took the ancient cloth in his weather-beaten hands, cradling it gently. A look of serenity swept his features, and his eyes sparkled. Turning to Marco, he enquired, "Can I wrap it around me?"

Marco looked over at Jack, who nodded.

The Norseman took the flag and gently wrapped it around his neck. His look of serenity changed abruptly, as the skin on his hands and face aged visibly. Startled, he began to unwrap the flag, but Marco stayed his hand.

"Think about it," he urged.

Trog paused, and left the flag as it was for a minute. His fair hair had turned sandy grey, then white, and his face sagged. But he was smiling. Then he removed the flag, folded it tenderly, and handed it back. There were tears in his eyes. He knelt down and looked at Jack.

"Bless you. Tonight I shall die."

Epilogue

Jack sat with the others around a huge bonfire late into the night. They had feasted well – the best meal Jack had had in a long time. It felt so strange to be back on the island, even though he'd only been gone a couple of days. And despite all the successes – bringing his father back alive, finding the third Shian treasure, disposing of Malevola and even defeating the Grey – it wasn't enough. He longed to get back to Edinburgh to finish off the job. Marco caught the look in his eyes.

"Take time to enjoy your victories, Jack. I know you've more to do, but the time for that has not yet come."

Jack looked over to where Fenrig and Morrigan sat. Ossian was seated next to Morrigan, and she was paying little attention to her brother.

"Your father will need a lot of care, but I believe he'll recover in time. Your grandfather – well, he's a tough old fox. Armina will have him right in a while."

"What about the Sphere?"

"You found it, and you were meant to find it. If that wasn't so, you'd never have got across the bridge, or got out of the Grey's cave. You knew that it showed the true path to someone who believed. Keep it for now."

"On the boat, I thought one of the McCools was going to take it. I'm not sure if I'm ready to look after it."

"Something tells me that it will be safe with you."

"I . . . I wanted to share it with Trog."

"That was gracious. You felt his pain. But you heard him bless you. He's happy just to have held it."

"Did he really mean it about dying tonight?" Jack wasn't sure why the old Norseman wasn't at the feast with everyone else.

"He's found the peace that has eluded him for so long," answered Marco. "Just wearing the flag for a minute was enough. You saw how he started to age when he put it round his neck? He knew then that he would die."

Jack thought how Trog had been startled by the change, but how he'd overcome his initial fear.

"Isn't he afraid?"

Marco smiled sadly. "He finally learned to forgive others – and to let others forgive him. He knows he will be gathered, and he's ready. He asked me to give you something."

Marco reached inside his cloak and withdrew Trog's long steel knife.

"In recognition of your generosity, and his release. It's his only real possession."

Tentatively, Jack took the knife from Marco. The knife that had dispatched the great swordfish of fortune. It seemed to glimmer in his hand.

"He had the knife so long, he believed it knew what to do. Maybe that will pass on to you. Guard it well."

Jack shrugged. "Are things on the mainland really so bad that we can't go home?"

"Pretty bad. The Kildashie are dragging many areas back to winter, more or less. And their takeover has given heart to Unseelie like the Thanatos all over. It will be hard times for the Seelie – and even the humans – for a while."

"What about Cos-Howe? Are the Claville crew still there?"

"The Kildashie have Cos-Howe surrounded – but they can last there for ages," he added, seeing Jack's look of dismay. "Cosmo and Henri know a thing or two about defending themselves."

"Have the Kildashie taken the Stone yet?"

"No, but they hold the Square, and are even in the Stone Room. The cabinet and the Stone's iron rings are keeping them at bay, though – for now."

"So how are we going to get home, then?"

"It will take time, and the most direct routes may not be open to you. You will need to be smart to take the Unseelie by surprise."

Time. It's always there, determining success and failure, thought Jack. Then he thought of the Kildashie . . . Thanatos . . . Red Caps . . . how could they possibly take that lot on?

"You have allies all over." Marco seemed to be reading Jack's mind. "But you'll need to collect them together before you can take the Unseelie on. And I think the McCools will stay; more may even join you."

"Did any of the other Congress members escape?"

"Not as far as we know. For the time being, all you have is

here on this island. But what you have is your family and good people around you. Never doubt the strength in that."

Jack looked round at the group. Rana and Lizzie were huddled in conversation. Aunt Dorcas was helping Uncle Hart to feed himself. Aunt Katie sat with Petros ... What about Uncle Doonya? What would the Thanatos do with him? Armina had allowed Grandpa to join the group for a while, but he limped badly.

Ossian's not much use – he can't keep his eyes off Morrigan. Only Finbogie's likely to be able to help if we need to do anything. Great.

"Don't despair, Jack. You've a long road ahead of you, but think how far you've come. You've found your father; you got Tamlina's ring back. And you have the *Mapa Mundi*. Think about it: the treasure that will show you your true path, if only you believe."

Jack fingered the flag that remained tied around his neck, and smiled.

I've got the Sphere.

He looked over to Petros, who waved back. Grandpa Sandy was looking over at Jack and gave a broad wink before resuming his conversation with Armina. Finbogie was in earnest conversation with Uncle Hart, but looked up at that moment and acknowledged Jack with a nod of the head. And Rana: she'd been great on the bridge, saving Grandpa's sceptre and helping to defeat the demons. Even dispatching Malevola.

"Now do you believe me, Jack?"

Jack untied the *Mapa Mundi* and held it out in front of him. As it formed into the Sphere, he scanned the two circles. What did they show?

An outline of the west coast of Scotland . . . falling leaves . . . and the north coast . . . some islands . . .

"You'll stay until the autumn," said Marco with a smile. "So you've several months yet – plenty of time."

In the second circle, a large earthen mound . . . and standing stones . . . and a growing crowd, people from lots of different countries by the look of them.

"Well?" Marco's tone was even.

"We've to meet up with others . . ." Jack's voice trailed off as he peered at the circles again. There was a bright low sun there . . . and snow. His brow furrowed.

"The midwinter sun," said Marco helpfully.

"But we don't go out during the winter," replied Jack innocently. "Everything's put on hold. For us, anyway: the Kildashie seem to like the cold."

"Then the Kildashie won't be expecting you."

Jack felt a tight knot in his stomach. A winter attack!

Read on for a sneak peek of Book 3 in
The Shian Quest Trilogy

JACK SHIAN
AND THE
DESTINY STONE

Coming Soon!

Prologue

Jack flung the stone into the rock pool as hard as he could. The splash soaked his shirt, but he didn't care. This waiting around was so *boring*.

Midsummer – now *that* had been exciting. Hunting the swordfish of fortune; finding the *Mapa Mundi*; raising the giant's bridge; defeating Malevola and the Grey; rescuing his father.

My father . . .

But he's still so weak, thought Jack; *all these years I've longed to find him, and it was two months before he could even talk. I still hardly know him.*

But I've got Tamlina's ring.

Jack took the ring from his Sintura belt and stared hard at the Triple-S spirals. What did they mean?

"Good things come in threes," Tamlina had said. Well, there were three spirals. Were they really the Destiny Stone, the Chalice, and the *Mapa Mundi*?

The sun glinted off the ring, and with a jolt Jack saw the spirals begin to turn. He felt a sudden whooshing sensation — like the low road, only faster. Instinctively he closed his eyes, but instead of the blur of shade and light of a low road journey, in his mind's eye Jack could see the street outside Cos-Howe in Edinburgh.

Two men, each tied to a chair, and facing each other. There's snow all around them, and a burning brazier next to one. The picture's blurred; I can't make out their faces . . . There are three tall men approaching . . . That's Boreus! And he's slapped one of the prisoners hard . . . Now he's holding the man's head so it faces sideways. Someone else is coming . . . He's put a sword in the fire. He's holding the hot blade up to the prisoner's eyes . . .

Bleeurgh! That's gross!

Jack opened his eyes and took a deep breath. He felt sick.

That was disgusting!

Jack shook his head, trying to clear the image seared into his mind, but it was no use. Like a film loop in his head, he kept seeing the sword slicing into eyes.

He puked.

1
Frustration

"What's the matter, Jack?" asked Rana.

Jack started, and wiped his mouth. Had she seen him puke? He wished his cousins wouldn't creep up on him like that. Glancing apprehensively at the ring, he noticed that one of the spiral arms had faded. He tried to concentrate.

"I thought I saw something. There was snow."

"Snow? What planet are you on? It's not even autumn yet."

"Shut up, Rana." Lizzie sounded concerned. "Jack doesn't look well."

"I'm alright. I was thinking about the Kildashie."

"That uncivilised bunch," snorted Lizzie. "It beats me how they can order the Thanatos around."

"It's the Tassitus charm," said Rana confidently. "If they can control sound, they can do what they want."

"And they're near the Stone too," added Jack. "That must make them stronger."

The Stone of Destiny. Jack hadn't seen it that many times, but he'd *known* it was giving power to the Shian square. Only now the Kildashie and the Thanatos were there, and they were torturing people.

I'd better not say anything about this to Dad. He's still not strong enough to handle this – whatever this *is.*

"More darrigs and dwarves have arrived," announced Rana. "There are some nearly every day now."

"This little one said he came from Lomond," said Lizzie. "It was freezing there."

"It's freezing wherever the Kildashie are," said Jack, thinking of the snow in his vision. "I wish we could do something to get them out. This island's getting crowded."

"You're just in a bad mood because you've had to start lessons again," mocked Rana. "Mum didn't waste any time getting you and Fenrig back to work when Gilmore arrived, did she?"

"It's not fair. Petros doesn't have any lessons. I've got to spend every morning stitching."

"At least that gets you away from his wife," pouted Rana. "Barassie's so *fussy*. All that stuff about what we can wear in the tents, what we can wear outside . . ."

"And all her rules about behaviour," interrupted Lizzie. "They're a pain. She never stops criticising."

"Gilmore's alright, I suppose," said Jack. "Good luck to anyone who escapes from the Kildashie. I just wish we were planning how to stop them getting the Destiny Stone and the Chalice."

"At least we've got the Sphere, the *Mapa Mundi*," said Lizzie. "They can't make the magycks complete until all three are together."

Jack smiled at the thought. He'd been the one to defeat the Nucklat and retrieve the Sphere. To begin with, Marco and Luka had even said he should keep it. But it had been an open secret that he had it, and each day Jack feared someone coming to steal it. All these Shian arriving on the island: maybe there were spies among them? In the end, Jack had entrusted the Sphere to Marco, but so far he'd kept Tamlina's ring. Tucked away in his Sintura belt, it was invisible, but people must know he had it . . . He'd got a strange buzz from it sometimes, but nothing like that vision . . .

That was an execution . . .

"Anyway," continued Rana, "the Sphere showed us leaving here in the autumn."

"I've never said I wanted summer to finish before," said Jack. "But Marco's season-wheel is turning so slowly. I just wish we could get on with it."

In his heart Jack knew that the Sphere had shown an autumn departure, but each week brought more news of Kildashie atrocities. Surely it was time to fight back?

"Can you tell me where Sandy of the Stone is?" A tall stranger had approached without any of them noticing.

Jack hurriedly thrust Tamlina's ring back into his Sintura belt. Had the man seen it?

"He'll be up at the house. Past those trees." Jack pointed; the man nodded and moved off.

"He's new, isn't he?" said Lizzie. "There are loads of people I don't recognise these days. D'you think we can trust them all?"

"You don't think he could be a Thanatos spy, do you?" asked Jack.

"I don't fancy meeting those Thanatos again," shuddered Lizzie. "You've never seen the unforgiven dead. Believe me, you don't want to."

"And there's Boaban Shee too," said Rana. "Mum told me they're like vampires. And there are Red Caps in the border lands. Most of the country's Unseelie now."

"It's hard to believe it's like winter almost everywhere," said Jack, looking up at the clear sky. "It's nice here. Bit cooler, though."

Jack resolved to give Tamlina's ring to Marco for safekeeping – for now. Like the *Mapa Mundi*, it was too much responsibility. And that vision had been scary.

"I bet Cos-Howe's doing OK, though." Jack tried to sound hopeful. "Cosmo can hold out as long as he wants."

"If the Thanatos . . ." Rana was silenced by a shove from her sister.

"Let's get back to the house," said Lizzie. "It's getting chilly."

The youngsters wandered along to Marco and Luka's house, surrounded as it now was by tents.

"Good news, kids," called out Aunt Dorcas. "Marco and Luka are coming back tonight."

"You mean the low road's open again?" Jack's eyes lit up.

"No, it's still out of action. Anyway, they hardly ever use it. Enda's bringing them over from the mainland."

"They're calling more McCools over too," added Aunt Katie.

Aunt Katie's changed in some ways, thought Jack. *More McCools must mean they're planning something, and once upon a time that would've got her frightened. But with Uncle Doonya a prisoner, she's not scared now, she's . . . determined.*

"Does that mean we're leaving soon?"

"You'll have to see what Marco says, Jack dear. A grig told us they'll be here this evening."

Grigs are flying again, even outside the low road. That definitely means things are on the move.

However, Jack's newfound optimism was to be short-lived. When Marco and Luka arrived that evening, all they would say was that the time was not yet right for a counter-attack. It wouldn't be long – *Where've I heard that before?* – but things had to be in place, otherwise the whole mission might fail.

Despite yet another "not yet", Jack was glad to see Marco and Luka again. Since midsummer they had hardly been on the island. And things on the mainland obviously hadn't improved. The Kildashie and the Thanatos had most Shian – few as they were – under the thumb. Stories of imprisonment, torture – even murder – were commonplace now. A few areas had managed to resist, but isolated and scattered, and with bitterly cold weather, this was not much use for a counter-attack.